Diversity, Equity, and Inclusion

Other Books of Related Interest

Opposing Viewpoints Series
Bias in Education
LGBTQIA+ Rights
Racial Discrimination and Criminal Justice

At Issue Series
Athlete Activism
Gender Politics
Male Privilege

Current Controversies Series
Microaggressions, Safe Spaces, and Trigger Warnings
Political Correctness
Reparations for Black Americans

> "Congress shall make no law … abridging the freedom of speech, or of the press."
>
> *First Amendment to the U.S. Constitution*

The basic foundation of our democracy is the First Amendment guarantee of freedom of expression. The Opposing Viewpoints series is dedicated to the concept of this basic freedom and the idea that it is more important to practice it than to enshrine it.

Diversity, Equity, and Inclusion

Andrew Karpan, Book Editor

Published in 2025 by Greenhaven Publishing, LLC
2544 Clinton Street,
Buffalo, NY 14224

Copyright © 2025 by Greenhaven Publishing, LLC

First Edition

All rights reserved. No part of this book may be reproduced in any form without permission in writing from the publisher, except by a reviewer.

Articles in Greenhaven Publishing anthologies are often edited for length to meet page requirements. In addition, original titles of these works are changed to clearly present the main thesis and to explicitly indicate the author's opinion. Every effort is made to ensure that Greenhaven Publishing accurately reflects the original intent of the authors. Every effort has been made to trace the owners of the copyrighted material.

Cover image: SeventyFour/Shutterstock.com

CataloginginPublication Data

Names: Karpan, Andrew, editor.
Title: Diversity, equity, and inclusion / edited by Andrew Karpan.
Description: First edition. | Buffalo, NY : Greenhaven Publishing, 2025. | Series: Opposing viewpoints | Includes bibliographical references and index.
Identifiers: ISBN 9781534509818 (pbk.) | ISBN 9781534509825 (library bound)
Subjects: LCSH: Diversity in the workplace. | Social responsibility of business. | Equity. | Cultural Diversity. | Cultural pluralism.
Classification: LCC HF5549.5.M5 D584 2025 | DDC 658.3008--dc23

Manufactured in the United States of America

Website: http://greenhavenpublishing.com

Contents

The Importance of Opposing Viewpoints	11
Introduction	14

Chapter 1: Have Diversity, Equity, and Inclusion Programs Positively Impacted Workplaces?

Chapter Preface	18
1. Is DEI Just Propaganda? *Kristen Parisi*	19
2. Diversity Initiatives Trap Workers of Color *Sheryl Nance-Nash*	24
3. DEI Leads to Happier Employees *Rita Men*	30
4. Employers Must Promote Inclusion, Not Just Diversity *Steven Smith, Katelynn Carter-Rogers, and Vurain Tabvuma*	35
5. Diverse Teams Are Smarter Teams *David Rock and Heidi Grant*	40
Periodical and Internet Sources Bibliography	45

Chapter 2: Does DEI Have a Positive Impact on Marginalized and Minority Groups?

Chapter Preface	48
1. Some Demographic Groups Value DEI More than Others *Rachel Minkin*	49
2. Diversity Programs Aren't Increasing Diversity *Frank Dobbin and Alexandra Kalev*	63
3. DEI Efforts Aren't Doing Enough to Help Workers with Disabilities *Stephen Friedman*	79

4. Racial Bias Is Still a Big Problem in Hiring Practices *Martin Abel*	84
Periodical and Internet Sources Bibliography	89

Chapter 3: Is DEI Under Attack?

Chapter Preface	92
1. Cutbacks and Legal Attacks Threaten DEI Initiatives *Andrea Hsu*	93
2. What Causes Resistance to DEI Initiatives? *Marcus Bright*	98
3. Against the DEI Industry *Kevin Wallsten*	104
4. Attacks on DEI Are Rooted in Racism *Tatishe Nteta, Adam Eichen, Douglas Rice, Jesse Rhodes, and Justin H. Gross*	112
5. Universities that Advertise Diversity Increase Racism *Arthur Scarritt*	118
Periodical and Internet Sources Bibliography	124

Chapter 4: Is True Diversity, Equity, and Inclusion Possible?

Chapter Preface	127
1. There Have Been Mixed Results in the Quest for More Diverse and Inclusive Workplaces *Sundiatu Dixon-Fyle, Kevin Dolan, Dame Vivian Hunt, and Sara Prince*	128
2. Merit Should Be Prioritized Over Diversity *Heather Mac Donald*	137
3. Global Health Equity Goes Beyond the Appearance of Diversity *Reya Farber*	142

4. There Are Many Advantages to Incorporating
   DEI in International Organizations **149**
   *William Newburry, Matevž (Matt) Rašković, Saba S.
   Colakoglu, Maria Alejandra Gonzalez-Perez, and Dana
   Minbaeva*

Periodical and Internet Sources Bibliography **161**

For Further Discussion **163**
Organizations to Contact **165**
Bibliography of Books **170**
Index **172**

The Importance of Opposing Viewpoints

Perhaps every generation experiences a period in time in which the populace seems especially polarized, starkly divided on the important issues of the day and gravitating toward the far ends of the political spectrum and away from a consensus-facilitating middle ground. The world that today's students are growing up in and that they will soon enter into as active and engaged citizens is deeply fragmented in just this way. Issues relating to terrorism, immigration, women's rights, minority rights, race relations, health care, taxation, wealth and poverty, the environment, policing, military intervention, the proper role of government—in some ways, perennial issues that are freshly and uniquely urgent and vital with each new generation—are currently roiling the world.

If we are to foster a knowledgeable, responsible, active, and engaged citizenry among today's youth, we must provide them with the intellectual, interpretive, and critical-thinking tools and experience necessary to make sense of the world around them and of the all-important debates and arguments that inform it. After all, the outcome of these debates will in large measure determine the future course, prospects, and outcomes of the world and its peoples, particularly its youth. If they are to become successful members of society and productive and informed citizens, students need to learn how to evaluate the strengths and weaknesses of someone else's arguments, how to sift fact from opinion and fallacy, and how to test the relative merits and validity of their own opinions against the known facts and the best possible available information. The landmark series Opposing Viewpoints has been providing students with just such critical-thinking skills and exposure to the debates surrounding society's most urgent contemporary issues for many years, and it continues to serve this essential role with undiminished commitment, care, and rigor.

The key to the series's success in achieving its goal of sharpening students' critical-thinking and analytic skills resides in its title—

Opposing Viewpoints. In every intriguing, compelling, and engaging volume of this series, readers are presented with the widest possible spectrum of distinct viewpoints, expert opinions, and informed argumentation and commentary, supplied by some of today's leading academics, thinkers, analysts, politicians, policy makers, economists, activists, change agents, and advocates. Every opinion and argument anthologized here is presented objectively and accorded respect. There is no editorializing in any introductory text or in the arrangement and order of the pieces. No piece is included as a "straw man," an easy ideological target for cheap point-scoring. As wide and inclusive a range of viewpoints as possible is offered, with no privileging of one particular political ideology or cultural perspective over another. It is left to each individual reader to evaluate the relative merits of each argument—as he or she sees it, and with the use of ever-growing critical-thinking skills—and grapple with his or her own assumptions, beliefs, and perspectives to determine how convincing or successful any given argument is and how the reader's own stance on the issue may be modified or altered in response to it.

This process is facilitated and supported by volume, chapter, and selection introductions that provide readers with the essential context they need to begin engaging with the spotlighted issues, with the debates surrounding them, and with their own perhaps shifting or nascent opinions on them. In addition, guided reading and discussion questions encourage readers to determine the authors' point of view and purpose, interrogate and analyze the various arguments and their rhetoric and structure, evaluate the arguments' strengths and weaknesses, test their claims against available facts and evidence, judge the validity of the reasoning, and bring into clearer, sharper focus the reader's own beliefs and conclusions and how they may differ from or align with those in the collection or those of their classmates.

Research has shown that reading comprehension skills improve dramatically when students are provided with compelling, intriguing, and relevant "discussable" texts. The subject matter of these collections could not be more compelling, intriguing, or urgently relevant to today's students and the world they are poised to inherit. The anthologized articles and the reading and discussion questions that are included with them also provide the basis for stimulating, lively, and passionate classroom debates. Students who are compelled to anticipate objections to their own argument and identify the flaws in those of an opponent read more carefully, think more critically, and steep themselves in relevant context, facts, and information more thoroughly. In short, using discussable text of the kind provided by every single volume in the Opposing Viewpoints series encourages close reading, facilitates reading comprehension, fosters research, strengthens critical thinking, and greatly enlivens and energizes classroom discussion and participation. The entire learning process is deepened, extended, and strengthened.

For all of these reasons, Opposing Viewpoints continues to be exactly the right resource at exactly the right time—when we most need to provide readers with the critical-thinking tools and skills that will not only serve them well in school but also in their careers and their daily lives as decision-making family members, community members, and citizens. This series encourages respectful engagement with and analysis of opposing viewpoints and fosters a resulting increase in the strength and rigor of one's own opinions and stances. As such, it helps make readers "future ready," and that readiness will pay rich dividends for the readers themselves, for the citizenry, for our society, and for the world at large.

Introduction

> "It is not our differences that divide us. It is our inability to recognize, accept, and celebrate those differences."
>
> —Audre Lorde, American writer, poet, philosopher, and civil rights leader

The first time the idea of affirmative action entered the rhetoric of the American politic was in an executive order signed in 1961 by President John F. Kennedy, which directed government contractors to "take affirmative action to ensure that applicants are employed and that employees are treated during employment without regard to their race, creed, color, or national origin."[1] Historically, this wasn't unprecedented; Kennedy's predecessor Dwight D. Eisenhower laid the groundwork for this by using similar powers to create a "Committee on Government Contracts" that furthered the idea that ". . . it is the obligation of the contracting agencies of the United States government and government contractors to insure compliance with, and successful execution of, the equal employment opportunity program of the United States government," according to text from a different executive order. [2] Later executive orders, like President Lyndon Johnson's 1965 order [3] were more direct, and the language of the Civil Rights Act, passed a year earlier, had established a similar framework for parts of the private sector.

More recently, however, the idea has been rebranded as "diversity, equity and inclusion (DEI)", a trio of words whose precise lexicographical origins are somewhat unclear, but that began gaining social currency in the years following the murder of George Floyd by police in 2020 and the popularity of the Black Lives Matter movement that followed. In part, this was because of various Supreme Court decisions that banned the outright use of categories like race, ethnicity, and gender in many hiring and admissions decisions. In the place of outright affirmative diversity programs, a bureaucratic web of nonprofit programs has been created to fill the gap left by the lack of officially sanctioned diversity programs and the general, collective idea that we ought to live in a more diverse world. Like so many social programs in the contemporary political era, instead of being carried out by public administrators, the project of diversity had been outsourced to the private sector. By some estimates, starting in 2020, companies around the world have spent $7.5 billion on DEI programs and the hiring of DEI officers throughout the corporate world. [4]

But this has not been without backlash. For political conservatives the programs became an easy scapegoat, and states like Florida passed laws that tried to curb the use of DEI programs in companies that used state funds. At the same time, the courts began filling up with lawsuits alleging corporate unfairness as a result of these programs, forcing programs to become smaller or even more circumspect. Even if unsuccessful, the lawsuits formed their own deterrent to diversity programs, implicitly raising the costs of implementation.

And criticism has come in other forms too. Were DEI programs working as intended, or had they become a form of corporate speak, an elevated performance of lip service with no actual changes in how corporations operate? As DEI infrastructure spread, it began to take new forms and move from country to country, facing the new trouble of adjusting itself for different demographics and different cultural contexts.

Nevertheless, diversity persists. By its own accord, the world is becoming less homogenized. More people are moving to new places and the demographic makeup of every institution will, by the implicit force of social change, eventually have to represent the changing world around them. In this way, concepts of diversity, equity, and inclusion will always be around, measuring and taking stock of those changes and the way they fit into the puzzled fabric of history.

The viewpoints in *Opposing Viewpoints: Diversity, Equity, and Inclusion* tackle that history and the ways it informs the changing textures of the present. The workforce is always changing—as is society—and DEI is just one measure of how.

Notes

[1] Executive Order 10925.
[2] Executive Order 10479
[3] Executive Order 11246
[4] "Affirmative Action Under Attack: How Did We Get Here?," *Washington Post*, March 9, 2024, https://www.washingtonpost.com/technology/interactive/2024/dei-history-affirmative-action-timeline/.

CHAPTER 1

Have Diversity, Equity, and Inclusion Programs Positively Impacted Workplaces?

Chapter Preface

The place where most DEI action happens is the workplace; as spaces of commerce, they operate under the umbrella of public regulation, discussion, and contemplation. But at the same time, companies are able to choose for themselves how to implement DEI programs—or whether to implement them at all—creating opportunities to test the possibilities of DEI.

In these viewpoints, writers look at how DEI programs have changed the workplace in the wake of a wave of discrimination lawsuits that started moving through the financial industry in the 1990s and have continued to this day. For some, the benefits of a more diverse workplace have become manifest. Others, however, are more skeptical.

Critics of DEI suggest that mandating a more diverse workplace has somehow not succeeded in creating one. The continuation of complaints suggests, perhaps, that underlying issues are not being addressed using the system's current tools for guiding the managerial world. The critics suggest that the larger issue is getting enough of a "buy-in" from the people involved, something that speaks to a more proactive, less mandatory approach, one with voluntary and enthusiastic participation.

These viewpoints showcase and occasionally try to tackle the ways in which diversity is regulated in the workplace.

VIEWPOINT 1

> "Musk's words aren't inconsequential, and could have ramifications beyond just creating a larger platform for DE&I dissent."

Is DEI Just Propaganda?

Kristen Parisi

This viewpoint by Kristen Parisi takes a look at what billionaire Elon Musk has to say about DEI programs. Parisi writes that Musk's comments signify the latest attack on the DEI industry, which had gained increased scrutiny over the previous year, largely coming from right-wing politicians. Parisi examines how Musk has become the figurehead for contempt toward DEI in mass culture and looks at how the anti-DEI movement has grown over the last few years. She suggests that some of those gestures, however, might be misguided. Kristen Parisi is a workplace reporter for Morning Brew, a news website that's run by the Insider brand.

As you read, consider the following questions:

1. Why does Elon Musk believe that DEI efforts are meant to punish a certain group of people?
2. What are some of the successes of the anti-DEI movement that this viewpoint points out?

"Elon Musk says diversity efforts are propaganda and 'DEI must die'" by Kristen Parisi. Morning Brew, Inc., December 20, 2023. Reprinted with permission.

3. Does this viewpoint ultimately agree or disagree with what Elon Musk says about DEI efforts?

Ladies and gentleman, the moment we've all been waiting for is here: Elon Musk has given his thoughts on DE&I.

The richest man in the world and owner of X (formerly Twitter) attacked diversity programs late Thursday night in a post, saying, "DEI must die." In a follow-up post on Dec. 16, Musk proclaimed, "'Diversity, Equity and Inclusion' are propaganda words for racism, sexism and other -isms. This is just as morally wrong as any other racism and sexism. Changing the target class doesn't make it right!"

> ## DEFINING DIVERSITY, EQUITY, AND INCLUSION
>
> ### What Is Equality?
> At its core, equality means fairness: we must ensure that individuals, or groups of individuals, are not treated less favourably because of their protected characteristics.
>
> Equality also means equality of opportunity: we must also ensure that those who may be disadvantaged can get the tools they need to access the same, fair opportunities as their peers.
>
> ### What Is Diversity?
> Diversity is recognizing, respecting and celebrating each other's differences. A diverse environment is one with a wide range of backgrounds and mindsets, which allows for an empowered culture of creativity and innovation.
>
> ### What Is Inclusion?
> Inclusion means creating an environment where everyone feels welcome and valued. An inclusive environment can only be created once we are more aware of our unconscious biases, and have learned how to manage them.

Musk may believe that DE&I efforts are meant to punish a certain group of people, but a DE&I expert explained how some dissenters ignore how equity and inclusion are built to help everyone succeed.

The latest. This is just the latest attack on an industry under increased scrutiny over the last year, largely from politicians.

A quick look at just some of the events that got us here:

- In 2022, Starbucks was sued for tying executive compensation to DE&I goals. The suit was ultimately dismissed as "frivolous" in August 2023.

What Are the Protected Characteristics?

The following are the legal protected characteristics, under The Equality Act 2010:

- Age
- Disability
- Gender reassignment
- Marriage and civil partnership
- Pregnancy and maternity
- Race
- Religion or belief
- Sex
- Sexual orientation

Discrimination on the grounds of any of these characteristics is illegal. Discrimination can take many forms including direct discrimination, indirect discrimination, bullying, harassment and victimization.

"What does equality, diversity, and inclusion mean," The University of Edinburgh School of Physics and Astronomy, June 14, 2022.

- In June, affirmative action in universities was deemed illegal by SCOTUS.
- America First Legal Foundation, which is run by former Trump advisor Stephen Miller, has sued several companies, including Kellogg's, Nordstrom, and Unilever, for their diversity practices in the last year.
- Billionaire Bill Ackman went after DE&I at universities in early December, claiming Harvard University's president was a so-called diversity hire.

Some politicians and business leaders (like Home Depot cofounder Bernard Marcus) brand organizations that deploy diversity efforts as "woke" and allege reverse discrimination. And while Musk claims to be against DE&I, his EV company, Tesla, releases an annual impact report and boasts that 67% of its employees are from underrepresented backgrounds.

Yes, but. Despite claims that DE&I strategies are harmful and encourage "reverse racism," the data shows that white men are still the majority in positions of corporate power. Jarvis Sam, founder of the Rainbow Disruption, a DE&I consultancy, and former chief diversity officer at Nike and Snap, said Musk's portrayal of DE&I could ultimately be used as a weapon for those in the traditional majority.

"When you're able to create a space where we put instructions of what DE&I does, or is meant to do, in such an elementary standard, that forces certain communities to believe that it is merely a social intervention that is meant to . . . somehow deny opportunity to the already highly represented majority population," Sam told HR Brew.

He also pointed out how Musk and other DE&I critics focus on representation, rather than equity and inclusion, something he suspects may allow them to feel as though the opportunity cards are now stacked against them.

"When we jump into inclusion, it is about creating a culture and an environment where everyone can thrive and feel a sense of psychological safety in the workplace," Sam explained. "That is a standard that is applicable to cisgendered, straight, white men, as much as it is to those that are the most marginalized amongst us."

Musk's words aren't inconsequential, and could have ramifications beyond just creating a larger platform for DE&I dissent. Employees at Tesla and other Musk-owned companies could be hurt as well.

"Someone like Elon Musk has to recognize the incredibly wide shadow that his words and sentiments capture," Sam said. "When you have an executive leader that's not demonstrating very clear accountability and conscientiousness around this . . . it can leave employees feeling incredibly unsupported, psychologically unsafe, and very challenged in their space."

Up next: Will Musk weigh in on why *Paw Patrol* will lead to society's downfall?

VIEWPOINT

> "It's wrong to assume that simply because someone identifies as BIPOC they are interested or qualified in doing equity, diversity and inclusion work. They may experience shame or resentment in this case."

Diversity Initiatives Trap Workers of Color

Sheryl Nance-Nash

In this viewpoint, Sheryl Nance-Nash reports on concerns from people of color regarding how workplaces have placed the burden of diversity efforts on them, a task that many people find stressful. For the people Nance-Nash talks to, having to perform in this way can feel like a "heavy lift" that often ends up feeling like "a tick-the-box-exercise." In turn, this creates its own atmosphere of fear, comparable in ways to the previous, more outwardly racialized social relationships. Sheryl Nance-Nash is a freelance writer whose work has been published by the BBC, Newsday, ABCNews.com, Black Enterprise, *and* Essence, *among others.*

As you read, consider the following questions:

1. What does this viewpoint say that many workplaces are still getting wrong about how they use diversity, equity, and inclusion programs?

"How corporate diversity initiatives trap workers of colour," by Sheryl Nance-Nash. BBC, September 14, 2020. Reprinted with permission.

2. What are some benefits that the author considers to be moves in the right direction?
3. What are some of the "knee-jerk solutions" that this viewpoint talks about and criticizes?

As companies around the world rush to implement diversity and inclusion programs, the burden to launch these initiatives are unduly falling on employees of color.

Amid the unsettling reality of the COVID-19 pandemic, another major epidemic has had global citizens reeling: racism. The deaths of Black Americans George Floyd, Breonna Taylor and Ahmaud Arbery ignited the Black Lives Matter movement in June, with protests that spread beyond U.S. borders and around the world.

In the wake of Black Lives Matter, companies across the globe have put new emphasis on diversity—adding people of color to their ranks, implementing bias training and attempting to lift marginalized voices. It's welcome news, but also a double-edged sword for people of color (POC) and Black, indigenous and people of color (BIPOC), as employers disproportionately lean on them to come up with initiatives, join committees and help formulate diversity game plans.

People of color are often tasked with this heavy lift while juggling their usual duties amid the coronavirus crisis—and not being offered additional compensation for the work. The burden also carries a high emotional price tag.

"It's not that [companies] don't know where else to turn—they are doing what's easiest and most convenient," says Shereen Daniels, managing director of HR Rewired, a London-based organization that facilitates anti-racist and equality workshops. She adds that many companies have not taken the time to acknowledge their own failings in this area, and instead have come up with knee-jerk solutions.

On the surface it looks like these organizations are taking meaningful action, but underneath, she says, they are treating diversity and inclusion as a tick-the box-exercise.

Stressed by the Spotlight

"Just as you wouldn't lean on a volunteer task force of employees to spearhead your compensation planning or finance operations, you shouldn't do the same with diversity, equity and inclusion," says Tara Johnson, a diversity consultant in New York. Yet many companies lean on—and even pressure—workers of color to raise their hands. In some cases, they even volunteer employees without their consent.

Daniels says she has heard numerous stories of workers of color being asked to write anti-racism statements; draft updated diversity, equity and inclusion strategies; sit in on meetings with board directors to sign off on communications; give the "POC view" on PR and marketing; and be available for any questions about "this Black stuff."

It's not just the expectation to take on more projects, however—it's an ongoing ask. Daniels also says that line managers have told people of color to be "on call" to answer any questions about Black Lives Matter, and help in whatever way they can. "Yet there is no conversation about how they are feeling, what support they need, if they are willing and able to help, how their workload will be adjusted accordingly and how they will be recognized. Organizations are metaphorically clicking their fingers and expecting POC to come running," says Daniels.

Some workers are angry and frustrated. "For years they have been ignored and their concerns swept under the carpet, and now these same leaders are tripping over themselves to get their views," she adds. And, in some organizations, people of color can also be penalized for non-participation.

Such tasks can cause stress and anxiety. Will workers of color face reprisals and repercussions if they speak the truth? How will they manage their increased workload if they take on new tasks?

Will they let down their colleagues of color if they don't step up to the task? Will these colleagues blame them if leadership doesn't follow through?

These are just some of the issues that can arise, says Stacie CC Graham, a London-based diversity, equity and inclusion trainer. "It's wrong to assume that simply because someone identifies as BIPOC they are interested or qualified in doing equity, diversity and inclusion work. They may experience shame or resentment in this case."

Beyond just the time that it takes to work on these projects, and the stress from carrying a workplace's burden, it's also onerous to educate others about the pain of systemic racial discrimination. Employers often make the mistake of not acknowledging that these initiatives are different and, in many ways, much harder than others, which increases the emotional burden for participants.

"It amounts to asking a person to relive his or her trauma, time and time again," says Rosalind Chow, associate professor of organizational behavior and theory at Carnegie Mellon University's Tepper School of Business in the U.S. city of Pittsburgh. "Leaders also haven't been thoughtful in ensuring the continued psychological safety of the employees who engage in this kind of 'emotional labor' for the company."

Lisa Kepinski, founder and director of the Inclusion Institute in Nesselwang, Germany, and co-author of the *Inclusion Nudges Guidebook*, says that involvement in these "extracurricular" corporate activities can have a negative impact on people of color, such as lower performance ratings, more stress, higher attrition and lower engagement. "These reflect the structural inequalities due to the framing of DEI [diversity, equity and inclusion] as a 'minority' thing," says Kepinski. This work can be seen as less important as a result.

Lip Service or Efficacy?

Although some companies aren't taking the right tack with their staff, others do seem to be making moves in the right direction.

David Rock, CEO and founder of the NeuroLeadership Institute, a New York City-based research organization focused on the science of leadership, works with major international companies on diversity and inclusion efforts. He says there are dozens of examples of organizations stepping up, with many donating significant sums to further equity efforts.

Of course, large-scale internal overhauls and major donations are helpful. But the organizations that have been—and will be—the most successful in helping to combat systemic racism do so in a way that's supportive, empowering and strategic.

"Effectiveness in diversity, equity and inclusion is similar to effectiveness in most organizational change initiatives or strategy—the key difference lies in implementation, through which you are able to gauge the sense of leadership and organizational commitment," says Dion Bullock, equity, inclusion and belonging strategy lead at Bravely, an online employee platform. The programs that have been most successful, he adds, are those that create processes that make everyone accountable for implementing the work; balance the program work and responsibility with an employee's main role; and compensate or recognize the work for advancement opportunities.

And, although companies have quickly been spinning up diversity programs with various approaches, their success will be contingent on the notion that combating systemic racism is not just a quarterly goal or a one-year initiative. "This work requires leaders to fundamentally rethink how their entire organization operates—how they design and share products and services, how they engage their customers, how they source and pay vendors, how they attract and grow talent, etc," says Bullock.

No doubt, there is a lot of talk—and results are yet to be seen. HR Rewired's Daniels is a bit sceptical of corporate programmes so far. "As for companies that are impressive, it's slim pickings I'm afraid. A lot are still making excuses and can't even write a statement or communicate with their teams. The ones who are doing something have at least held listening forums and are building ally-ship programs. I think it's too early to give any gold stars."

Rock agrees that it's premature to start handing out accolades, but says that "it is easy for employees to work out how 'real' [a company's] commitment is." "When employees, especially people of color, notice a true commitment to investing internally and externally, this is likely to be intrinsically rewarding, by activating an increase in their sense of fairness—one of the big drivers of motivation in the brain."

'Only Say Yes If You Want To'

Amid all of the doom and gloom about people of color being asked to participate in these programs, it's important to point out that, in some cases, workers benefit from getting involved.

For those who want to take on the labor, there's potential upside of increased leadership, responsibility and voice, says Thomas Sasso, an assistant professor with the department of management at the Gordon S Lang School of Business and Economics at the University of Guelph in Ontario. "If there is trust that the organization will engage meaningfully in this process, this can increase organizational commitment, job satisfaction, organizational-citizenship behaviors and other positive employee and organizational outcomes."

So, if you're a person of color being tapped to contribute? Make sure you have details and for how much you'll be expected to contribute, address logistics concerns around your existing work and know who else is on your team. And, most importantly, only say yes if you want to, advises Natasha Aruliah, consultant and coach on social justice, equity, diversity and inclusion in Vancouver. "If you're uncomfortable or it's not in your wheelhouse, don't do it."

VIEWPOINT 3

> "Overall, our study supports the notion that employees still value and appreciate their companies' focus on diversity, equity and inclusion efforts."

DEI Leads to Happier Employees

Rita Men

In this viewpoint Rita Men examines recent studies—including her own—on how diversity, equity, and inclusion initiatives impact workplaces. Research shows that DEI programs have positive impacts on productivity, creativity, innovation, and organization, and that most workers appreciate when their employers have a DEI program. Employees feel more engaged at companies where their employers talk about diversity and equity. Emphasizing DEI helps employees feel valued and included which, in turn, leads to better workplace performances and higher profits. Rita Men is a professor of public relations and director of Internal Communication Research at the University of Florida.

"Workers Like It When Their Employers Talk About Diversity and Inclusion," by Rita Men, The Conversation August 30, 2023, https://theconversation.com/workers-like-it-when-their-employers-talk-about-diversity-and-inclusion-208727. Licensed under CC BY-ND 4.0 International.

Have Diversity, Equity, and Inclusion Programs Positively Impacted Workplaces?

As you read, consider the following questions:

1. According to a 2021 survey cited in this viewpoint, what percent of chief human resources officers consider DEI a top priority?
2. According to this viewpoint, are the benefits of DEI limited to companies in the U.S.?
3. What is the relationship between workplace engagement and having an employer that discusses diversity and inclusion for racial minority employees?

Many companies have made commitments toward diversity, equity and inclusion initiatives in recent years, particularly since the murder of George Floyd sparked weeks of racial justice riots in 2020.

But some of those efforts, such as hiring diversity leaders and creating policies to address racial inequality, have stalled or reversed at the same time as a growing conservative backlash is threatening to further undermine such initiatives.

Most recently, a June 2023 Supreme Court ruling tossing out affirmative action policies at several universities has prompted businesses and advocates to worry that similar corporate efforts to improve the diversity of their workforces may be next.

That would be bad news for companies, because research has shown that diversity, equity and inclusion initiatives improve creativity, innovation, productivity and organizational performance.

What's more, a majority of workers say they want their employers to do DEI. My own research in corporate communications suggests how employees communicate their efforts is just as important as having them.

DEI and the Workplace

Diversity, equity and inclusion are three related values that companies and other organizations use to guide their efforts to create workplaces that are welcoming to people from all walks of life. These values emphasize the respect of individual differences and fair treatment of all people, regardless of race, gender, age, sexual orientation or other factors.

The implementation of DEI measures varies across organizations, with strategies ranging from policies that ensure the fair treatment of workers of color to training and the establishment of employee resource groups, which are internal communities built around workers' shared identities or interests. Examples include networks for women, people of color or veterans.

While strategies may vary, DEI is in wide use across corporate America. Every Fortune 100 company listed some kind of DEI initiative on its website as of July 2022, and a 2021 survey found that 82% of chief human resource officers said DEI was their foremost concern.

Broad Benefits of DEI

Numerous studies on diversity, equity and inclusion policies have found them to have many positive impacts on corporate performance.

Consulting company McKinsey in May 2020 reviewed data on over 1,000 companies in 15 countries and found that the "business case for inclusion and diversity is stronger than ever."

Its analysis showed that in 2019 companies in the top quartile in terms of ethnic and cultural diversity were 36% more likely to report above-average profits than those at the bottom, slightly better than in 2014. And companies with the most gender diversity among executives were 25% more likely to outperform the market, up from 15% in 2014.

A 2019 study that analyzed workforce diversity in the U.S. federal government found that racial diversity is significantly and positively related to organizational performance.

One of the reasons DEI initiatives have a positive impact is because workers appreciate them. For example, a survey conducted in early 2023 found that most employees—56%—think it's a good thing if their company is focused on DEI.

Talking Up DEI

But my own work suggests that getting many of these benefits from DEI initiatives may depend on how well employers are communicating their efforts to workers. In 2021, colleagues Sunny Qin, Renee Mitson, Patrick Thelen and I conducted an online survey with 657 full-time employees across 27 industries in the U.S. We published the findings in June 2023.

We asked respondents how well they thought their employers communicated around the topic of diversity, including efforts to promote a diverse workforce. We also assessed participants' engagement in their companies as well as the employees' cultural intelligence, or the ability to interact and adapt across cultures. We then used a statistical technique called structural equation modeling analysis to spot relationships between all their answers.

We found that the employees who worked for companies that talked more about their commitment to fostering a diverse and inclusive environment were also more engaged in their work. This was also correlated with higher levels of cultural intelligence, and together they contributed to a more inclusive work environment.

Importantly, we found that this effect was strongest for racial minorities, whose level of engagement was more highly correlated with how well their employer created an inclusive climate than for white people in our survey.

Valued and Included

Overall, our study supports the notion that employees still value and appreciate their companies' focus on diversity, equity and inclusion efforts.

And as we found, a more diverse and inclusive work environment leads to a more engaged workforce when companies continually

Diversity, Equity, and Inclusion

communicate about their stance, values and commitment to DEI. Such communications signal to employees that their employers hear their voices and stand with them.

Having a diverse and inclusive workplace isn't just about checking off boxes. It's about making sure everyone feels valued and included.

VIEWPOINT 4

> *"Scholars have called for a shift in emphasis from studying diversity in the workplace to studying inclusion in the workplace, arguing that although diversity and inclusion are interrelated concepts, they are distinct."*

Employers Must Promote Inclusion, Not Just Diversity

Steven Smith, Katelynn Carter-Rogers, and Vurain Tabvuma

In this viewpoint Steven Smith, Katelynn Carter-Rogers, and Vurain Tabvuma talk about how many businesses tend to focus on the "diversity" part of DEI while ignoring the "inclusion" part, which can cause DEI programs to be unsustainable or even backfire. This is because workplaces that only focus on having diverse employees but do not focus on making them feel included have a difficult time sustaining diversity. Policies, procedures, and actions at all levels of these companies need to focus on including a diverse range of employees, and differences among employees must be celebrated. The authors then offer three suggestions for how to effectively promote inclusivity in the workplace. Steven Smith is a professor of psychology at Saint Mary's University in Nova Scotia, Canada,

"Diversity in the Workplace Isn't Enough: Businesses Need to Work Toward Incluion," by Steven Smith, Katelynn Carter-Rogers, and Vurain Tabvuma, The Conversation, November 27, 2022, https://theconversation.com/diversity-in-the-workplace-isnt-enough-businesses-need-to-work-toward-inclusion-194136. Licensed under CC BY-ND 4.0 International.

Diversity, Equity, and Inclusion

where Vurain Tabvuma is an associate professor in the Sobey School of Business Management. Katelynn Carter-Rogers is an assistant professor of management and Indigenous business at St. Francis Xavier University, also in Nova Scotia.

As you read, consider the following questions:

1. What is another name for DEI used in this viewpoint?
2. What three suggestions do the authors offer for creating an inclusive workplace?
3. According to the authors, what should employee onboarding include?

Diversity is now widely believed to be good for business. In the corporate world, it's often referred to as Equity, Diversity, Inclusion and Accessibility (EDIA) or Diversity, Equity and Inclusion (DEI) training or awareness.

Not surprisingly, there is now a desire across all sectors to understand how organizations can harness diversity and inclusion to increase employee performance and well-being. Yet workplace diversity programs can often be ineffective, or even backfire. And when they do work, some programs can be unsustainable.

Why does this happen? One reason is that, despite best intentions and companies wanting to hire diverse employees, organizations are often not equipped or ready to adapt their work environment to sustain diversity.

This can lead to conflict within organizations, as well as a lack of belonging and acceptance by the new employees hired. In other words, the employees may be diverse, but they do not feel included. Employees who do not feel included are less likely to stay.

Inclusion Goes Beyond Diversity

Perhaps it is not a surprise, then, that scholars have called for a shift in emphasis from studying *diversity* in the workplace to studying *inclusion* in the workplace, arguing that although diversity and inclusion are interrelated concepts, they are distinct.

How is inclusion different from diversity? Defining features of inclusive climates are reflected in policies, procedures and actions at all levels of an organization. Inclusive organizations are consistent with fair treatment of everyone, with a deliberate focus on groups that historically have fewer opportunities and who are still stigmatized within our society.

Importantly, inclusion goes beyond diversity. Differences among individuals are not just identified, but are celebrated and integrated into daily work life. These differences are also woven into the organization's culture through policies, climate, leadership and practices.

Fundamentally, an inclusive climate is a diverse environment within an organization that values the contribution of all employees. It is a workplace climate where people with different beliefs, perceptions and observable characteristics are able to work effectively with others, feel valued, and have strong feelings of belonging within that organizational context.

This begs the question: How does an organization create an inclusive workplace?

All Voices Must Be Heard

Members of the majority may feel targeted by EDIA programs and can have concerns about "reverse discrimination," leading to conflict within the group. If majority group members end up feeling "passed over," they could become resentful and create an unwelcoming, negative work environment for new hires who may be perceived as under-qualified.

To combat this, organizations need to understand both the experiences of the minority and majority within an organization. Organizations must ensure that barriers and concerns are understood, and proactive steps towards inclusion are taken. Employers need to understand their current workplace climate and learn what practices need to be addressed and implemented into their organization's culture.

Harness the Power of Inclusive Leaders

Managers are responsible for creating inclusion in the workplace. They must: show that they are comfortable with diversity; alter the rules of acceptable behavior to adapt to the new culture; create opportunities for dialogue about and across differences; demonstrate an interest in authentic (and in some cases learning *to be* authentic) diversity; and encourage authenticity in others.

Recent research shows that a leader's pro-diversity beliefs, humility and cognitive complexity increase the likelihood of inclusive behaviours, which in turn, has positive behavioural outcomes related to job performance, creativity and reduced turnover rates.

Intentional and Involved Decision-Making

It is important to start with the end in mind. Inclusive practices should begin at the very moment newcomers to an organization begin their tenure. There is a positive relationship between employee workplace onboarding and organizational commitment, job satisfaction, and job performance. Employee onboarding also reduces quitting intentions.

New employee onboarding should not only focus on orientating newcomers to the organization, but is also a chance to familiarize newcomers with its inclusive practices and communicate that their unique beliefs, perceptions and characteristics are welcome and valued.

In situations where new hires may be the only person coming from a specific group of people, navigating the workplace becomes difficult and can feel exclusionary. Having access to mentors and colleagues with similar lived experience is beneficial for transition and overall retention.

Shared Responsibility

It's important to understand that, although these workplace attitudes and behaviors can shed light on how new employees relate to their workplaces, they don't tell us how much new employees feel they can participate in decision-making, or how welcoming, healthy, and safe their work environment is. There is always work to be done to improve workplace culture.

Inclusion is everyone's responsibility and doesn't end after the hiring stage. If organizations truly want to retain diverse employees and have them be successful, they need to make consistent and sustained efforts to support the integration of these employees in the workplace.

The goal of EDIA programs is to help organizations develop an inclusive organizational climate and design employee onboarding training that focuses on the employees' sense of belonging and well-being. A truly inclusive approach needs to create an inclusive climate, have inclusive leaders and implement inclusive practices.

VIEWPOINT 5

> "People from diverse backgrounds might actually alter the behavior of a group's social majority in ways that lead to improved and more accurate group thinking."

Diverse Teams Are Smarter Teams
David Rock and Heidi Grant

In this viewpoint, David Rock and Heidi Grant make the case that more diverse workplaces in the corporate world are a good thing for the bottom line too, in addition to reflecting widely held social values. Striving to increase workplace diversity is not an empty slogan, the pair argue. Instead, it's a way to modernize workplaces. They present data supporting their argument that embracing new viewpoints makes workplaces better at reexamining facts and remaining more objective than the segregated workplaces of the past. This argument makes a case for actively breaking up workplace homogeneity. David Rock is cofounder of a group called the Neuroleadership Institute and author of Your Brain at Work. Heidi Grant is a social psychologist who works for the Motivation Science Center at Columbia Business School.

"Why Diverse Teams Are Smarter" by David Rock and Heidi Grant. Harvard Business Review, November 4, 2016. Reprinted with permission.

Have Diversity, Equity, and Inclusion Programs Positively Impacted Workplaces?

As you read, consider the following questions:

1. Why does this viewpoint argue that diverse teams are more likely to constantly reexamine facts and remain objective?
2. Does data suggest that diverse teams outperform homogenous ones?
3. What do the authors of this viewpoint mean by "joint intellectual potential"?

Striving to increase workplace diversity is not an empty slogan—it is a good business decision. A 2015 McKinsey report on 366 public companies found that those in the top quartile for ethnic and racial diversity in management were 35% more likely to have financial returns above their industry mean, and those in the top quartile for gender diversity were 15% more likely to have returns above the industry mean.

In a global analysis of 2,400 companies conducted by Credit Suisse, organizations with at least one female board member yielded higher return on equity and higher net income growth than those that did not have any women on the board.

In recent years a body of research has revealed another, more nuanced benefit of workplace diversity: nonhomogenous teams are simply smarter. Working with people who are different from you may challenge your brain to overcome its stale ways of thinking and sharpen its performance. Let's dig into why diverse teams are smarter.

They Focus More on Facts

People from diverse backgrounds might actually alter the behavior of a group's social majority in ways that lead to improved and more accurate group thinking. In a study published in the *Journal of Personality and Social Psychology*, scientists assigned 200 people to six-person mock jury panels whose members were either all white or included four white and two Black participants. The people were shown a video of a trial of a Black defendant and white victims. They then had to decide whether the defendant was guilty.

It turned out that the diverse panels raised more facts related to the case than homogenous panels and made fewer factual errors while discussing available evidence. If errors did occur, they were more likely to be corrected during deliberation. One possible reason for this difference was that white jurors on diverse panels recalled evidence more accurately.

Other studies have yielded similar results. In a series of experiments conducted in Texas and Singapore, scientists put financially literate people in simulated markets and asked them to price stocks. The participants were placed in either ethnically diverse or homogenous teams. The researchers found that individuals who were part of the diverse teams were 58% more likely to price stocks correctly, whereas those in homogenous groups were more prone to pricing errors, according to the study, published in the journal *PNAS*.

Diverse teams are more likely to constantly reexamine facts and remain objective. They may also encourage greater scrutiny of each member's actions, keeping their joint cognitive resources sharp and vigilant. By breaking up workplace homogeneity, you can allow your employees to become more aware of their own potential biases—entrenched ways of thinking that can otherwise blind them to key information and even lead them to make errors in decision-making processes.

They Process Those Facts More Carefully

Greater diversity may also change the way that entire teams digest information needed to make the best decisions. In a study published in the *Personality and Social Psychology Bulletin*, Katherine Phillips of Northwestern University and her team divided sorority or fraternity members into four-member groups, each of which had to read interviews conducted by a detective investigating a murder. Three people in every group, referred to as "oldtimers" in the study, came from the same sorority or fraternity, whereas the fourth, the so-called "newcomer," was either a member of the same sorority or fraternity or a different one. The three oldtimers in each group gathered to decide who was the most likely murder suspect. Five minutes into their discussion, the newcomer joined the deliberation and expressed their opinion as to who the suspect was.

It turned out that although groups with out-group newcomers felt less confident about the accuracy of their joint decisions, they were more likely to guess who the correct suspect was than those with newcomers who belonged to the same group.

The scientists think that diverse teams may outperform homogenous ones in decision making because they process information more carefully. Remember: considering the perspective of an outsider may seem counterintuitive, but the payoff can be huge.

They're Also More Innovative

To stay competitive, businesses should always continue to innovate. One of the best ways to boost their capacity to transform themselves and their products may involve hiring more women and culturally diverse team members, research suggests. In a study published in *Innovation: Management, Policy & Practice*, the authors analyzed levels of gender diversity in research and development teams from 4,277 companies in Spain. Using statistical models, they found that companies with more women were more likely to introduce radical new innovations into the market over a two-year period.

In another study, published in *Economic Geography*, the authors concluded that increased cultural diversity is a boon to innovativeness. They pooled data on 7,615 firms that participated in the London Annual Business Survey, a questionnaire conducted with the UK capital's executives that asks a number of questions about their companies' performance. The results revealed that businesses run by culturally diverse leadership teams were more likely to develop new products than those with homogenous leadership.

Though you may feel more at ease working with people who share your background, don't be fooled by your comfort. Hiring individuals who do not look, talk, or think like you can allow you to dodge the costly pitfalls of conformity, which discourages innovative thinking.

In a nutshell, enriching your employee pool with representatives of different genders, races, and nationalities is key for boosting your company's joint intellectual potential. Creating a more diverse workplace will help to keep your team members' biases in check and make them question their assumptions. At the same time, we need to make sure the organization has inclusive practices so that everyone feels they can be heard. All of this can make your teams smarter and, ultimately, make your organization more successful, whatever your goals.

Periodical and Internet Sources Bibliography

The following articles have been selected to supplement the diverse views presented in this chapter.

Nicholas Confessore, "'America Is Under Attack': Inside the Anti-D.E.I. Crusade," the *New York Times*, January 20, 2024. https://www.nytimes.com/interactive/2024/01/20/us/dei-woke-claremont-institute.html.

Todd Corley, Vontrese "Voni" Pamphile, and Katina Sawyer, "What Has (and Hasn't) Changed About Being a Chief Diversity Officer," *Harvard Business Review*, September 23, 2022. https://hbr.org/2022/09/what-has-and-hasnt-changed-about-being-a-chief-diversity-officer.

Conor Friedersdorf, "The DEI Industry Needs to Check Its Privilege," the *Atlantic*, May 31, 2023. https://www.theatlantic.com/ideas/archive/2023/05/dei-training-initiatives-consultants-companies-skepticism/674237.

Roxane Gay, "What's My D.E.I. Training? My Own Life," the *New York Times*, February 4, 2024. https://www.nytimes.com/2024/02/04/business/dei-job-interview.html.

Emma Goldberg, "Facing Backlash, Some Corporate Leaders Go 'Under the Radar' With D.E.I.," *New York Times*, January 22, 2024. https://www.nytimes.com/2024/01/22/business/diversity-backlash-fortune-500-companies.html.

Ryan Grim and Tema Okun, "Tema Okun on Her Mythical Paper on White Supremacy," the Intercept, February 3, 2023. https://theintercept.com/2023/02/03/deconstructed-tema-okun-white-supremacy.

Emily Peck, "DEI Backlash Hits Corporate America," Axios, November 27, 2023. https://www.axios.com/2023/11/27/dei-affirmative-action-supreme-court.

Bridget Read, "Doing the Work at Work: What Are Companies Desperate for Diversity Consultants Actually Buying?" *New York Magazine*, May 26, 2021. https://www.thecut.com/article/diversity-equity-inclusion-industrial-companies.html.

Diversity, Equity, and Inclusion

Kelefa Sanneh, "The Limits of 'Diversity,'" the *New Yorker*, October 2, 2017. https://www.newyorker.com/magazine/2017/10/09/the-limits-of-diversity.

Keeanga-Yamahtta Taylor, "The Campaign Against D.E.I.," the *New Yorker*, January 22, 2024. https://www.newyorker.com/news/our-columnists/the-campaign-against-dei.

Lily Zheng, "The Failure of the DEI-Industrial Complex," *Harvard Business Review*, December 1, 2022. https://hbr.org/2022/12/the-failure-of-the-dei-industrial-complex.

CHAPTER 2

Does DEI Have a Positive Impact on Marginalized and Minority Groups?

Chapter Preface

Who could be against diversity? While the larger concept of "diversity, equity, and inclusion" incorporates ideas that date to the civil rights era of the 1960s, today the phrase can feel somewhat generic, like a placeholder for the very notion of commonly held values. The history of how those ideas became part of the firmament of contemporary thought is, itself, the history of centuries of social change.

And yet, even these basic concepts can feel fraught and under attack, as they have become stand-ins for the reality of changing demographics and, perhaps, a change in the social order as well, a move away from the status quo. In this way, these ideas have landed in the crosshairs of reactionary elements, at home and in politics, whether in the form of angry podcasters, opinionated billionaires, or the president of the United States.

For those reasons too, these programs have also been a playground for contemporary discourse around race itself. When the footage of the killing of George Floyd sent shockwaves around the country and the world in 2020, it was precisely these programs that were turned to in order to provide some kind of answers for what ought to be done. As representatives of modern values, diversity, equity, and inclusion have become part of how events are processed and the way in which individuals and organizations choose to respond to injustices. But do these programs actually benefit the marginalized and minority groups they're intended to help, or are they simply intended to help organizations look better? Whether or not these initiatives are effective in a concrete sense or merely symbolic is hotly debated.

VIEWPOINT 1

> "Men and women have different views on the impact gender has on a person's ability to succeed where they work."

Some Demographic Groups Value DEI More than Others

Rachel Minkin

In this viewpoint, Rachel Minkin discusses a Pew Research Center report on data they've collected on the subject of DEI initiatives in the workplace. According to this viewpoint, they talked to 5,902 U.S. workers to get these observations and found that demographics matter in opinions about DEI. Rachel Minkin, who wrote up the summary of the findings for the research center, observes in this viewpoint that partisan differences continue to be the dominating force in determining where people stand on these issues. Rachel Minkin is a research associate focusing on social and demographic trends at Pew Research Center.

As you read, consider the following questions:

1. According to this viewpoint, how do attitudes toward DEI efforts differ between Democrats and Republicans?
2. How do the racial demographics split on approval for DEI programs?

"Diversity, Equity and Inclusion in the Workplace" by Rachel Minkin, Pew Research Center, May 17, 2023. Reprinted with permission.

Diversity, Equity, and Inclusion

3. Where do the individuals surveyed in this viewpoint land on how well their workplaces are handling DEI?

Workplace diversity, equity and inclusion efforts, or DEI, are increasingly becoming part of national political debates. For a majority of employed U.S. adults (56%), focusing on increasing DEI at work is a good thing, according to a new Pew Research Center survey. But opinions about DEI vary considerably along demographic and political lines.

Most workers have some experience with DEI measures at their workplace. About six-in-ten (61%) say their company or organization has policies that ensure fairness in hiring, pay or promotions, and 52% say they have trainings or meetings on DEI at work. Smaller shares say their workplace has a staff member who promotes DEI (33%), that their workplace offers salary transparency (30%), and that it has affinity groups or employee resource groups based on a shared identity (26%). Majorities of those who have access to these measures say each has had a positive impact where they work.

This nationally representative survey of 5,902 U.S. workers, including 4,744 who are not self-employed, was conducted Feb. 6-12, 2023, using the Center's American Trends Panel. The survey comes at a time when DEI efforts are facing some backlash and many major companies are laying off their DEI professionals.

Some key findings from the survey:

- Relatively small shares of workers place a lot of importance on diversity at their workplace. About 3-in-10 say it is extremely or very important to them to work somewhere with a mix of employees of different races and ethnicities (32%) or ages (28%). Roughly a quarter say the same about having a workplace with about an equal mix of men and women (26%) and 18% say this about a mix of employees of different sexual orientations.

Does DEI Have a Positive Impact on Marginalized and Minority Groups?

- More than half of workers (54%) say their company or organization pays about the right amount of attention to increasing DEI. Smaller shares say their company or organization pays too much (14%) or too little attention (15%), and 17% say they're not sure. Black workers are more likely than those in other racial and ethnic groups to say their employer pays too little attention to increasing DEI. They're also among the most likely to say focusing on DEI at work is a good thing (78% of Black workers say this), while White workers are the least likely to express this view (47%).
- Women are more likely than men to value DEI at work. About 6-in-10 women (61%) say focusing on increasing DEI at work is a good thing, compared with half of men. And larger shares of women than men say it's extremely or very important to them to work at a place that is diverse when it comes to gender, race and ethnicity, age, and sexual orientation.
- There are wide partisan differences in views of workplace DEI. Most Democratic and Democratic-leaning workers (78%) say focusing on DEI at work is a good thing, compared with 30% of Republicans and Republican leaners. Democrats are also far more likely than Republicans to value different aspects of diversity. And by wide margins, higher shares of Democrats than Republicans say the policies and resources related to DEI available at their workplace have had a positive impact.
- Half of workers say it's extremely or very important to them to work somewhere that is accessible for people with physical disabilities. About 3-in-10 workers (29%) say this is somewhat important to them, and 21% say it's not too or not at all important. A majority of workers (76% among those who do not work fully remotely) say their workplace is at least somewhat accessible for people with physical disabilities.
- Many say being a man or being White is an advantage where they work. The survey asked respondents whether a person's gender, race or ethnicity makes it easier or harder to be successful where they work. Shares ranging from 45% to 57%

say these traits make it neither easier nor harder. But far more say being a man and being White makes it easier than say it makes it harder for someone to be successful. Conversely, by double-digit margins, more say being a woman, being Black or being Hispanic makes it harder than say it makes it easier to be successful where they work.

The Value of DEI Efforts at Work

A majority of workers (56%) say focusing on increasing diversity, equity and inclusion at work is mainly a good thing; 28% say it is neither good nor bad, and 16% say it is a bad thing. Views on this vary along key demographic and partisan lines.

Half or more of both men and women say focusing on increasing DEI at work is a good thing, but women are more likely than men to offer this view (61% vs. 50%). In turn, men are more than twice as likely as women to say it is a bad thing (23% vs. 9%).

About two-thirds or more of Black (78%), Asian (72%) and Hispanic (65%) workers say that focusing on DEI at work is a good thing. Among White workers, however, fewer than half (47%) say it's a good thing; in fact, 21% say it's a bad thing. But there are wide partisan, gender and age gaps among White workers, with majorities of White Democrats, women and those under age 30 saying focusing on DEI at work is a good thing.

Workers under 30 are the most likely age group to say focusing on DEI at work is a good thing. About two-thirds (68%) of workers ages 18 to 29 say this, compared with 56% of workers 30 to 49, 46% of those 50 to 64, and 52% of those 65 and older.

Views also differ by educational attainment, with 68% of workers with a postgraduate degree saying focusing on DEI at work is a good thing, compared with 59% of those with a bachelor's degree only and 50% of those with some college or less education.

Democratic and Democratic-leaning workers are much more likely to say focusing on DEI at work is a good thing (78%) than to say it is a bad thing (4%) or that it is neither good nor bad (18%). Views among Republican and Republican-leaning workers are more mixed: Some 30% say focusing on DEI at work is a good thing, while the same share (30%) say it's a bad thing, and 39% say it's neither good nor bad.

A Majority of Workers Say Their Employer Pays the Right Amount of Attention to DEI

When it comes to the focus of their own employer, 54% of workers say their company or organization pays about the right amount of attention to increasing diversity, equity and inclusion. The remainder are divided between saying their employer pays too much (14%) or too little attention (15%), or that they're not sure (17%).

Women are more likely than men to say their employer pays too little attention to increasing DEI (17% vs. 12%). In turn, men are more likely than women to say too much attention is paid to this where they work (18% vs. 10%).

Black workers (28%) are the most likely to say their company or organization pays too little attention to increasing DEI, compared with smaller shares of White (11%), Hispanic (19%) and Asian (17%) workers who say the same.

Views on this question also differ by party. While half or more of both Republican and Democratic workers say their company or organization pays the right amount of attention to DEI, Democrats are more likely than Republicans to say their employer pays too little attention to it (21% vs. 7%). In turn, Republicans are more likely than Democrats to say their employer pays too much attention to DEI (24% vs. 6%).

The Importance of a Diverse Workforce

While a majority of workers say focusing on increasing diversity, equity and inclusion at work is a good thing, relatively small shares place great importance on working at a place that is diverse when it comes to gender, race and ethnicity, age, and sexual orientation. About 3-in-10 workers say it's extremely or very important to them to work somewhere with a mix of employees of different races and ethnicities (32%) and ages (28%), while 26% say the same about having about an equal mix of men and women. And 18% say this about having a mix of employees of different sexual orientations at their workplace.

Women are more likely than men to say it's extremely or very important to them to work at a place that is diverse across all measures asked about in the survey. For example, there are 11 percentage point differences in the shares of women compared with men saying it is extremely or very important to them to work somewhere that has a mix of employees of different races and ethnicities (37% vs. 26%) and about an equal mix of men and women (31% vs. 20%).

Black workers are among the most likely to value racial, ethnic and age diversity in the workplace. Some 53% of Black workers say it is extremely or very important to them to work somewhere with a mix of employees of different races and ethnicities, compared with 39% of Hispanic workers and 25% of White workers who say the same; 43% of Asian workers say this is important to them. (There is no statistically significant difference between the share of Asian workers and the shares of Black and Hispanic workers who hold this view.) And while 42% of Black workers highly value working somewhere with a mix of employees of different ages, smaller shares of Hispanic (33%), Asian (30%) and White (24%) workers say the same.

When it comes to diversity of sexual orientation, 28% of Black workers and 22% of Hispanic workers say it is extremely or very important to them to work somewhere that is diverse in this way; 15% each among White and Asian workers say the same.

Workers under age 50 are more likely than those 50 and older to say racial and ethnic diversity in their workplace is extremely or very important to them (35% vs. 26%). Workers younger than 50 are also more likely to say having about an equal mix of men and women is important to them, with workers ages 18 t0 29 the most likely to say this (34% vs. 26% of workers 30 to 49, and 20% each among those 50 to 64 and 65 and older).

There are also differences by educational attainment, with larger shares of workers with a postgraduate degree than those with less education saying it's extremely or very important to them that their workplace is diverse across all measures asked about in the survey. For example, 44% of workers with a postgraduate degree say having a mix of employees of different races and ethnicities is extremely or very important to them, compared with 34% of those with a bachelor's degree only and 27% of those with some college or less.

Democratic workers are much more likely than Republican workers to say working somewhere that is diverse when it comes to gender, race and ethnicity, age, and sexual orientation is extremely or very important to them. In fact, about half of Democrats (49%) place great importance on having a mix of employees of different races and ethnicities where they work, compared with 13% of Republicans. And there are differences of at least 20 points between the shares of Democrats and Republicans saying it's extremely or very important to them to work somewhere that has about an equal mix of men and women (39% of Democrats say this vs. 12% of Republicans) and a mix of employees of different ages (39% vs. 17%) and sexual orientations (27% vs. 7%).

Overall, a majority of workers say their workplace has a mix of employees of different ages (58% say this describes their current workplace extremely or very well). Smaller shares say their workplace has about an equal mix of men and women (38%) and a mix of employees of different races and ethnicities (46%) and sexual orientations (28%). These assessments do not vary much across demographic groups.

Half of Workers Place Great Importance on Working at a Place that Is Accessible for People with Physical Disabilities

Half of workers say it is extremely or very important to them to work somewhere that is accessible for people with physical disabilities; 29% say it is somewhat important and 21% say it is not too or not at all important to them.

Highly valuing an accessible workplace varies by gender, race and ethnicity, and party, but there is no significant difference in responses between those who do and don't report having a disability.

About 6-in-10 women (58%) say it is extremely or very important to them that their workplace is accessible, compared with 41% of men.

Black workers are more likely than workers of other racial and ethnic groups to place great importance on their workplace being accessible: 62% of Black workers say this is extremely or very important, compared with 51% of Hispanic, 48% of White and 43% of Asian workers.

A majority of Democrats (59%) say it is extremely or very important to them to work somewhere that is accessible for people with physical disabilities; 40% of Republican say the same. Some 27% of Republicans say this is not too or not at all important to them, compared with 15% of Democrats.

There is no statistically significant difference in the shares of workers who have a disability and those who do not saying it is extremely or very important to them to work somewhere that is accessible for people with physical disabilities. But workers who do not have a disability are more likely than those who do to say this is not too or not at all important to them (21% vs. 15%).

Among those who don't work fully remotely, about three-quarters of workers (76%) say their workplace is at least somewhat accessible for people with physical disabilities, with 51% saying it is extremely or very accessible. Some 17% say their workplace is not too or not at all accessible, and 8% are not sure.

DEI Measures and Their Impact

When asked whether the company or organization they work for has a series of measures that are typically associated with diversity, equity and inclusion efforts, a majority of workers say their employer has policies that ensure everyone is treated fairly in hiring, pay or promotions (61%), and 52% say there are trainings or meetings on DEI where they work.

Does DEI Have a Positive Impact on Marginalized and Minority Groups?

Smaller shares say their workplace has a staff member whose main job is to promote DEI at work (33%), a way for employees to see the salary range for all positions (30%), and groups created by employees sometimes known as affinity groups or employee resource groups (ERGs) based on shared identities such as gender, race or being a parent (26%).

Responses do not vary much by most demographic characteristics. However, workers with at least a bachelor's degree are consistently more likely than those with less education to say each of these five measures is available where they work.

Workers Tend to See Positive Impact from Policies and Resources Associated with DEI Where They Work

Among those whose workplace offers each policy or resource, a majority of workers say each measure has had a somewhat or very positive impact where they work. About a third or fewer workers say each resource has had neither a positive nor negative impact, and about 1-in-10 or fewer say each of these has had a somewhat or very negative impact.

Democrats and Republicans are about equally likely to say their workplace has these measures in place, but Democrats are more likely than Republicans to say the impact of each has been positive by margins ranging from 10 to 32 points (among those who say their workplace has these measures). For example, 66% of Democrats who say their workplace has a way for employees to see the salary range for all positions say this has had a somewhat or very positive impact, compared with 56% of Republicans who say this. And while about three-quarters of Democrats (74%) say having a staff member whose main job is to promote DEI at work has had a positive impact, fewer than half of Republicans (42%) say the same.

Women are more likely than men to say each of these policies and resources has had a very or somewhat positive impact where they work. This is mainly driven by gender differences among Republicans: There are double-digit differences in the shares of Republican women and Republican men who say many of these resources have had a positive impact. For example, 58% of Republican women say having a staff member whose main job is to promote DEI at work has had at least a somewhat positive impact where they work, compared with 31% of Republican men who hold this view. The same share of Republican women (58%) say having affinity groups or ERGs has had a positive impact, compared with 38% of Republican men who say the same.

Among Democrats, majorities of both men and women offer positive assessments of these resources in their workplace, but Democratic women are more likely than Democratic men to say having trainings or meetings on DEI at work have had a positive impact (72% vs. 65%).

While there are differences by race, ethnicity and age on overall attitudes about DEI in the workplace, there are no consistent differences along these dimensions in how workers with access to these policies and resources at their workplace assess their impact.

About Half of Workers Who Have Participated in DEI Trainings in the Last Year Say They've Been Helpful

Out of all workers, about 4-in-10 (38%) have participated in a DEI training in the last year. A similar share (40%) did not participate or say their workplace does not offer these trainings, and 21% are not sure if their employer offers these trainings.

Looking only at those whose company or organization has trainings or meetings on DEI, about three-quarters (73%) say they have participated in such trainings in the past year. And assessments of these trainings tend to be positive, with 53% of workers who've participated saying they were very or somewhat helpful. About a third (34%) give a more neutral assessment, saying the trainings were neither helpful nor unhelpful, and 13% say they were very or somewhat unhelpful.

While men and women are about equally likely to have participated in trainings on DEI in the past year, women are more

Does DEI Have a Positive Impact on Marginalized and Minority Groups?

likely than men to say the trainings have been at least somewhat helpful (60% vs. 46%).

Republicans and Democrats are also equally likely to say they've participated in these trainings in the past year, but Democrats are far more likely than Republicans to say the trainings have been helpful (66% vs. 36%). About one-in-five Republicans say they've been unhelpful (19%), compared with 9% of Democrats.

While both Democratic men and women offer similar assessments of the DEI trainings they've participated in, there are gender differences among Republican workers. Republican women are more likely than Republican men to say the trainings they've participated in have been helpful (47% vs. 28%). Conversely, 22% of Republican men, compared with 14% of Republican women, say the trainings have been unhelpful.

Few Workers Are Members of Affinity Groups or ERGs at Work

While 26% of workers say there are affinity groups or employee resource groups (ERGs) where they work, members of these groups account for a very small share of workers overall. Just 6% of workers say they are members of an affinity group or ERG, with 58% of workers saying these groups are either not available at their workplace or that they aren't a member. Another 37% say they are not sure if their workplace offers these groups.

Among workers who say there are affinity groups or ERGs at their workplace, 22% say they are personally a member. Women are more likely than men to be members of these groups (28% vs. 16%). And 28% of non-White workers say they are a member of an affinity group or ERG, compared with 18% of White workers.

How Gender, Race and Ethnicity Impact Success in the Workplace

When asked about the impact a person's gender, race or ethnicity has on their ability to succeed at work, workers tend to say these characteristics neither make it easier nor harder to be successful at their workplace.

Still, when it comes to gender, workers are more likely to say being a man makes it easier to be successful where they work than to say it makes it harder (36% vs. 6%). In contrast, a larger share says being a woman makes it harder to be successful than say it makes it easier (28% vs. 11%).

Men and women have different views on the impact gender has on a person's ability to succeed where they work. Some 44% of women say being a man makes it at least a little easier to be successful, including 24% who say it makes it a lot easier. This compares with 29% of men who say being a man makes it at least a little easier to be successful.

Similarly, 34% of women say being a woman makes it harder to be successful where they work, compared with 21% of men.

Women under age 50 are especially likely—more so than women ages 50 and older or men in either age group—to say being a man makes it easier to be successful where they work and that being a woman makes it harder. For example, 38% of women ages 18 to 49 say being a woman makes it harder to be successful where they work. This compares with 29% of women 50 and older, 25% of men younger than 50, and an even smaller share of men 50 and older (13%).

When it comes to views about how race or ethnicity affects people's ability to succeed at work, 51% of Black workers say being Black makes it harder to be successful where they work. This is significantly higher than the shares of Asian (41%), Hispanic (23%) and White (18%) workers who say the same about the impact of being Black.

Similarly, about 4-in-10 Asian workers (39%) say being Asian makes it harder to be successful in their workplace, a higher share than workers of other racial and ethnic groups who say the same about being Asian.

Hispanic, Black and Asian workers are about equally likely to say being Hispanic makes it harder to be successful where they work. A smaller share of White workers say the same about being Hispanic.

When asked about the impact of being White in their workplace, workers across racial and ethnic groups are more likely to say it makes it easier than to say it makes it harder to be successful. This is especially the case among Black and Asian workers. About half of Black (52%) and Asian (51%) workers say being White makes it easier to be successful where they work, compared with 37% of Hispanic and 24% of White workers who say the same about being White.

Previously released findings from this survey found that Black workers are more likely than White, Hispanic and Asian workers to report that they have experienced discrimination or have been treated unfairly by an employer in hiring, pay or promotions because of their race or ethnicity at some point in their careers (though not necessarily where they currently work). Women are also more likely than men to say they've experienced such discrimination because of their gender.

There are large partisan gaps in views of whether gender, race or ethnicity make it easier or harder to be successful at work. Some 47% of Democratic workers say being a man makes it at least somewhat easier to be successful at their workplace, compared with 25% of Republican workers. Democrats are also more likely than Republicans to say being a woman makes it harder to succeed (37% vs. 17%).

Democratic and Republican women are more likely than their male counterparts to say being a woman makes it harder—and being a man makes it easier—to be successful where they work. The differences between Republican women and Republican men are particularly striking. About a quarter of Republican women (26%) say being a woman makes it harder to be successful, compared with 10% of Republican men. And while 36% of Republican women say being a man makes it easier to be successful where they work, just 16% of Republican men say the same.

Democratic workers are more than three times as likely as Republican workers to say being White makes it easier to succeed where they work (48% vs. 13%), and they are also more likely than Republicans to say being Black, Hispanic or Asian makes it harder. About 4-in-10 Democrats (39%) say being Black makes it harder for someone to succeed at their workplace, compared with just 9% of Republicans. Similarly, 30% of Democrats say being Hispanic makes it harder to succeed, compared with 8% of Republicans. And while smaller shares in both parties say being Asian makes it harder to succeed, Democrats are more likely than Republicans to say this (16% vs. 6%). These partisan differences remain when looking only at Democrats and Republicans who are White.

VIEWPOINT 2

> "It turns out that while people are easily taught to respond correctly to a questionnaire about bias, they soon forget the right answers."

Diversity Programs Aren't Increasing Diversity

Frank Dobbin and Alexandra Kalev

In this viewpoint, Frank Dobbin and Alexandra Kalev make the case that workplace diversity programs have largely failed to improve the overall diversity among the managerial set in the corporate world after they were instituted in that sector following a series of high-profile lawsuits in the late 1990s and early 2000s. The authors make the case that a lot of "popular solutions" to diversity problems among senior executives have largely "backfired," citing reports that claim that "managerial ranks of white women and all minority groups except Hispanic men decline" in workplaces that try to adopt formal grievance systems. Instead, this viewpoint makes the case for using ideas that purportedly do not focus on controlling and regulating workplaces, but instead are more affirmative, like a recruitment program. Frank Dobbin is a sociology professor at Harvard University and Alexandra Kalev is a sociology professor at Tel Aviv University in Israel.

"Why Diversity Programs Fail" by Frank Dobbin and Alexandra Kalev, Harvard Business Review, 2016. Reprinted with permission.

Diversity, Equity, and Inclusion

As you read, consider the following questions:

1. Why does this viewpoint make the case that diversity programs have become "tools that are designed to preempt lawsuits" instead of actually increasing diversity in workplaces?
2. What are the problems, according to this viewpoint, with just outlawing bias?
3. According to this viewpoint, what impact does hiring tests have on workplace diversity?

Businesses started caring a lot more about diversity after a series of high-profile lawsuits rocked the financial industry. In the late 1990s and early 2000s, Morgan Stanley shelled out $54 million—and Smith Barney and Merrill Lynch more than $100 million each—to settle sex discrimination claims. In 2007, Morgan was back at the table, facing a new class action, which cost the company $46 million. In 2013, Bank of America Merrill Lynch settled a race discrimination suit for $160 million. Cases like these brought Merrill's total 15-year payout to nearly half a billion dollars.

It's no wonder that Wall Street firms now require new hires to sign arbitration contracts agreeing not to join class actions. They have also expanded training and other diversity programs. But on balance, equality isn't improving in financial services or elsewhere. Although the proportion of managers at U.S. commercial banks who were Hispanic rose from 4.7% in 2003 to 5.7% in 2014, white women's representation dropped from 39% to 35%, and Black men's from 2.5% to 2.3%. The numbers were even worse in investment banks (though that industry is shrinking, which complicates the analysis). Among all U.S. companies with 100 or more employees, the proportion of Black men in management increased just slightly—from 3% to 3.3%—from 1985 to 2014. White women saw bigger gains from 1985 to 2000—rising from 22% to 29% of managers—but their numbers haven't budged since then. Even in Silicon Valley, where many leaders tout the need to increase diversity for both business and social justice reasons, bread-and-butter tech jobs remain dominated by white men.

It shouldn't be surprising that most diversity programs aren't increasing diversity. Despite a few new bells and whistles, courtesy of big data, companies are basically doubling down on the same approaches they've used since the 1960s—which often make things worse, not better. Firms have long relied on diversity training to reduce bias on the job, hiring tests and performance ratings to limit it in recruitment and promotions, and grievance systems to give employees a way to challenge managers. Those tools are designed to preempt lawsuits by policing managers' thoughts and actions. Yet laboratory studies show that this kind of force-feeding can activate bias rather than stamp it out. As social scientists have found, people often rebel against rules to assert their autonomy. Try to coerce me to do X, Y, or Z, and I'll do the opposite just to prove that I'm my own person.

In analyzing three decades' worth of data from more than 800 U.S. firms and interviewing hundreds of line managers and executives at length, we've seen that companies get better results when they ease up on the control tactics. It's more effective to engage managers in solving the problem, increase their on-the-job contact with female and minority workers, and promote social accountability—the desire to look fair-minded. That's why interventions such as targeted college recruitment, mentoring programs, self-managed teams, and task forces have boosted diversity in businesses. Some of the most effective solutions aren't even designed with diversity in mind.

Here, we dig into the data, the interviews, and company examples to shed light on what doesn't work and what does.

Why You Can't Just Outlaw Bias

Executives favor a classic command-and-control approach to diversity because it boils expected behaviors down to dos and don'ts that are easy to understand and defend. Yet this approach also flies in the face of nearly everything we know about how to motivate people to make changes. Decades of social science research point to a simple truth: You won't get managers on board by blaming and shaming them with rules and reeducation. Let's look at how the most common top-down efforts typically go wrong.

Diversity training. Do people who undergo training usually shed their biases? Researchers have been examining that question since before World War II, in nearly a thousand studies. It turns out that while people are easily taught to respond correctly to a questionnaire about bias, they soon forget the right answers. The positive effects of diversity training rarely last beyond a day or two, and a number of studies suggest that it can activate bias or spark a backlash. Nonetheless, nearly half of midsize companies use it, as do nearly all the Fortune 500.

Many firms see adverse effects. One reason is that three-quarters use negative messages in their training. By headlining the legal case for diversity and trotting out stories of huge settlements, they issue an implied threat: "Discriminate, and the company will pay the price." We understand the temptation—that's how we got your attention in the first paragraph—but threats, or "negative incentives," don't win converts.

Another reason is that about three-quarters of firms with training still follow the dated advice of the late diversity guru R. Roosevelt Thomas Jr. "If diversity management is strategic to the organization," he used to say, diversity training must be mandatory, and management has to make it clear that "if you can't deal with that, then we have to ask you to leave." But five years after instituting required training for managers, companies saw no improvement in the proportion of white women, Black men, and Hispanics in management, and the share of Black women actually decreased by 9%, on average, while the ranks of Asian American men and women shrank by 4% to 5%. Trainers tell us that people often respond to compulsory courses with anger and resistance—and many participants actually report more animosity toward other groups afterward.

But voluntary training evokes the opposite response ("I chose to show up, so I must be pro-diversity"), leading to better results: increases of 9% to 13% in Black men, Hispanic men, and Asian American men and women in management five years out (with no decline in white or Black women). Research from the University of Toronto reinforces our findings: In one study white subjects read a brochure critiquing prejudice toward Blacks. When people felt pressure to agree with it, the reading strengthened their bias against Blacks. When they felt the choice was theirs, the reading reduced bias.

Companies too often signal that training is remedial. The diversity manager at a national beverage company told us that the top brass uses it to deal with problem groups. "If there are a number of complaints . . . or, God forbid, some type of harassment case . . . leaders say, 'Everyone in the business unit will go through it again.'" Most companies with training have special programs for managers. To be sure, they're a high-risk group because they make the hiring, promotion, and pay decisions. But singling them out implies that they're the worst culprits. Managers tend to resent that implication and resist the message.

Hiring tests. Some 40% of companies now try to fight bias with mandatory hiring tests assessing the skills of candidates for frontline jobs. But managers don't like being told that they can't hire whomever they please, and our research suggests that they often use the tests selectively. Back in the 1950s, following the postwar migration of Blacks northward, Swift & Company, Chicago meatpackers, instituted tests for supervisor and quality-checking jobs. One study found managers telling Blacks that they had failed the test and then promoting whites who hadn't been tested. A Black machine operator reported: "I had four years at Englewood High School. I took an exam for a checker's job. The foreman told me I failed" and gave the job to a white man who "didn't take the exam."

This kind of thing still happens. When we interviewed the new HR director at a West Coast food company, he said he found that white managers were making only strangers—most of them minorities—take supervisor tests and hiring white friends without testing them. "If you are going to test one person for this particular job title," he told us, "you need to test everybody."

But even managers who test everyone applying for a position may ignore the results. Investment banks and consulting firms build tests into their job interviews, asking people to solve math and scenario-based problems on the spot. While studying this practice, Kellogg professor Lauren Rivera played a fly on the wall during hiring meetings at one firm. She found that the team paid little attention when white men blew the math test but close attention when women and Blacks did. Because decision-makers (deliberately or not) cherry-picked results, the testing amplified bias rather than quashed it.

Managers made only strangers—most of them minorities—take tests and hired white friends without testing them.

Companies that institute written job tests for managers—about 10% have them today—see decreases of 4% to 10% in the share of managerial jobs held by white women, African American men and women, Hispanic men and women, and Asian American women over the next five years. There are significant declines among white and Asian American women—groups with high levels of education, which typically score well on standard managerial tests. So group differences in test-taking skills don't explain the pattern.

Performance ratings. More than 90% of midsize and large companies use annual performance ratings to ensure that managers make fair pay and promotion decisions. Identifying and rewarding the best workers isn't the only goal—the ratings also provide a litigation shield. Companies sued for discrimination often claim that their performance rating systems prevent biased treatment.

But studies show that raters tend to lowball women and minorities in performance reviews. And some managers give everyone high marks to avoid hassles with employees or to keep their options open when handing out promotions. However managers work around performance systems, the bottom line is that ratings don't boost diversity. When companies introduce them, there's no effect on minority managers over the next five years, and the share of white women in management drops by 4%, on average.

Grievance procedures. This last tactic is meant to identify and rehabilitate biased managers. About half of midsize and large firms have systems through which employees can challenge pay, promotion, and termination decisions. But many managers—rather than change their own behavior or address discrimination by others—try to get even with or belittle employees who complain. Among the nearly 90,000 discrimination complaints made to the Equal Employment Opportunity Commission in 2015, 45% included a charge of retaliation—which suggests that the original report was met with ridicule, demotion, or worse.

Once people see that a grievance system isn't warding off bad behavior in their organization, they may become less likely to speak up. Indeed, employee surveys show that most people don't report discrimination. This leads to another unintended consequence: managers who receive few complaints conclude that their firms don't have a problem. We see this a lot in our interviews. When we talked with the vice president of HR at an electronics firm, she mentioned the widely publicized "difficulties other corporations are having" and added, "We have not had any of those problems . . . we have gone almost four years without any kind of discrimination complaint!" What's more, lab studies show that protective measures like grievance systems lead people to drop their guard and let bias affect their decisions, because they think company policies will guarantee fairness.

Things don't get better when firms put in formal grievance systems; they get worse. Our quantitative analyses show that the managerial ranks of white women and all minority groups except Hispanic men decline—by 3% to 11%—in the five years after companies adopt them.

Still, most employers feel they need some sort of system to intercept complaints, if only because judges like them. One strategy that is gaining ground is the "flexible" complaint system, which offers not only a formal hearing process but also informal mediation. Since an informal resolution doesn't involve hauling the manager before a disciplinary body, it may reduce retaliation. As we'll show, making managers feel accountable without subjecting them to public rebuke tends to help.

Tools for Getting Managers on Board

If these popular solutions backfire, then what can employers do instead to promote diversity?

A number of companies have gotten consistently positive results with tactics that don't focus on control. They apply three basic principles: engage managers in solving the problem, expose them to people from different groups, and encourage social accountability for change.

Engagement. When someone's beliefs and behavior are out of sync, that person experiences what psychologists call "cognitive dissonance." Experiments show that people have a strong tendency

DEI Positively Impacts Productivity

DE&I programs are uprooting old mindsets by removing subconscious biases while hiring, such as race or ethnicity-based biases, sexism, and other archaic prejudices. Instead, it replaces them with more useful and modern philosophies and tools, making way for a huge number of benefits. Research shows that employees are 60% as productive as they could be in their workplace. Some of the factors that contribute to this are: lack of sense of belonging, workplace stress, lack of recognition, and toxic workplace behavior.

Studies show that work-related stress affects minorities in particular. There are many reasons for this, such as different levels of education attained and poor treatment by management. A good DE&I program would help sensitize both management and employees, and help them learn how to interact with employees in a more inclusive way. It would also help minority employees feel more comfortable in their environment and more included and accepted, leading to a boost in employee productivity by almost a 40%!

to "correct" dissonance by changing either the beliefs or the behavior. So, if you prompt them to act in ways that support a particular view, their opinions shift toward that view. Ask them to write an essay defending the death penalty, and even the penalty's staunch opponents will come to see some merits. When managers actively help boost diversity in their companies, something similar happens: They begin to think of themselves as diversity champions.

Take college recruitment programs targeting women and minorities. Our interviews suggest that managers willingly participate when invited. That's partly because the message is positive: "Help us find a greater variety of promising employees!" And involvement is voluntary: Executives sometimes single out managers they think would be good recruiters, but they don't drag anyone along at gunpoint.

Managers who make college visits say they take their charge seriously. They are determined to come back with strong candidates

> ### DE&I Helps Identify, Attract and Retain Top Talent
>
> DE&I initiatives help in creating authentic connections with existing employees, who can then recommend other qualified individuals to fill vacant positions. Such recommendations help find the right fit, both in terms of skills and organizational culture. It's also helpful in retaining employees. Employees who feel they are undervalued, treated poorly, and have fewer growth opportunities are the most likely to leave a company. In the U.S., numerous studies show that white males are more likely to get a promotion than their BIPOC and/or female counterparts. Therefore, a DE&I program will help build long-lasting bonds among employees, and help management understand their needs better while aiding in breaking the glass ceiling for many.
> [...]
>
> "Leadership Coaching Group/DE&I (Diversity, Equity & Inclusion) delivers more impact than you see!" by Numly.

from underrepresented groups—female engineers, for instance, or African American management trainees. Cognitive dissonance soon kicks in—and managers who were wishy-washy about diversity become converts.

The effects are striking. Five years after a company implements a college recruitment program targeting female employees, the share of white women, Black women, Hispanic women, and Asian American women in its management rises by about 10%, on average. A program focused on minority recruitment increases the proportion of Black male managers by 8% and Black female managers by 9%.

Mentoring is another way to engage managers and chip away at their biases. In teaching their protégés the ropes and sponsoring them for key training and assignments, mentors help give their charges the breaks they need to develop and advance. The mentors then come to believe that their protégés merit these opportunities—whether they're white men, women, or minorities. That is cognitive dissonance—"Anyone I sponsor must be deserving"—at work again.

While white men tend to find mentors on their own, women and minorities more often need help from formal programs. One reason, as Georgetown's business school dean David Thomas discovered in his research on mentoring, is that white male executives don't feel comfortable reaching out informally to young women and minority men. Yet they are eager to mentor assigned protégés, and women and minorities are often first to sign up for mentors.

Mentoring programs make companies' managerial echelons significantly more diverse: On average they boost the representation of Black, Hispanic, and Asian American women, and Hispanic and Asian American men, by 9% to 24%. In industries where plenty of college-educated nonmanagers are eligible to move up, like chemicals and electronics, mentoring programs also increase the ranks of white women and Black men by 10% or more.

Only about 15% of firms have special college recruitment programs for women and minorities, and only 10% have mentoring programs. Once organizations try them out, though, the upside becomes clear. Consider how these programs helped Coca-Cola in the wake of a race discrimination suit settled in 2000 for a record $193 million. With guidance from a court-appointed external task force, executives in the North America group got involved in recruitment and mentoring initiatives for professionals and middle managers, working specifically toward measurable goals for minorities. Even top leaders helped to recruit and mentor, and talent-sourcing partners were required to broaden their recruitment efforts. After five years, according to former CEO and chairman Neville Isdell, 80% of all mentees had climbed at least one rung in management. Both individual and group mentoring were open to all races but attracted large numbers of African Americans (who accounted for 36% of protégés). These changes brought important gains. From 2000 to 2006, African Americans' representation among salaried employees grew from 19.7% to 23%, and Hispanics' from 5.5% to 6.4%. And while African Americans and Hispanics respectively made up 12% and 4.9% of professionals and middle managers in 2002, just four years later those figures had risen to 15.5% and 5.9%.

This began a virtuous cycle. Today, Coke looks like a different company. This February, *Atlanta Tribune* magazine profiled 17 African American women in VP roles and above at Coke, including CFO Kathy Waller.

Contact. Evidence that contact between groups can lessen bias first came to light in an unplanned experiment on the European front during World War II. The U.S. army was still segregated, and only whites served in combat roles. High casualties left General Dwight Eisenhower understaffed, and he asked for Black volunteers for combat duty. When Harvard sociologist Samuel Stouffer, on leave at the War Department, surveyed troops on their racial attitudes, he found that whites whose companies had been joined by Black platoons showed dramatically lower racial animus and greater willingness to work alongside Blacks than those whose companies remained segregated. Stouffer concluded that whites fighting alongside Blacks came to see them as soldiers like themselves first and foremost. The key, for Stouffer, was that whites and Blacks had to be working toward a common goal as equals—hundreds of years of close contact during and after slavery hadn't dampened bias.

Business practices that generate this kind of contact across groups yield similar results. Take self-managed teams, which allow people in different roles and functions to work together on projects as equals. Such teams increase contact among diverse types of people, because specialties within firms are still largely divided along racial, ethnic, and gender lines. For example, women are more likely than men to work in sales, whereas white men are more likely to be in tech jobs and management, and Black and Hispanic men are more likely to be in production.

As in Stouffer's combat study, working side-by-side breaks down stereotypes, which leads to more equitable hiring and promotion. At firms that create self-managed work teams, the share of white women, Black men and women, and Asian American women in management rises by 3% to 6% over five years.

Rotating management trainees through departments is another way to increase contact. Typically, this kind of cross-training allows people to try their hand at various jobs and deepen their understanding of the whole organization. But it also has a positive impact on diversity, because it exposes both department heads and trainees to a wider variety of people. The result, we've seen, is a bump of 3% to 7% in white women, Black men and women, and Asian American men and women in management.

About a third of U.S. firms have self-managed teams for core operations, and nearly four-fifths use cross-training, so these tools are already available in many organizations. Though college recruitment and mentoring have a bigger impact on diversity—perhaps because they activate engagement in the diversity mission and create intergroup contact—every bit helps. Self-managed teams and cross-training have had more positive effects than mandatory diversity training, performance evaluations, job testing, or grievance procedures, which are supposed to promote diversity.

Social accountability. The third tactic, encouraging social accountability, plays on our need to look good in the eyes of those around us. It is nicely illustrated by an experiment conducted in Israel. Teachers in training graded identical compositions attributed to Jewish students with Ashkenazic names (European heritage) or with Sephardic names (African or Asian heritage). Sephardic students typically come from poorer families and do worse in school. On average, the teacher trainees gave the Ashkenazic essays Bs and the Sephardic essays Ds. The difference evaporated, however, when trainees were told that they would discuss their grades with peers. The idea that they might have to explain their decisions led them to judge the work by its quality.

In the workplace you'll see a similar effect. Consider this field study conducted by Emilio Castilla of MIT's Sloan School of Management: a firm found it consistently gave African Americans smaller raises than whites, even when they had identical job titles and performance ratings. So Castilla suggested transparency to activate social accountability. The firm posted each unit's average performance rating and pay raise by race and gender. Once managers realized that employees, peers, and superiors would know which parts of the company favored whites, the gap in raises all but disappeared.

Corporate diversity task forces help promote social accountability. CEOs usually assemble these teams, inviting department heads to volunteer and including members of underrepresented groups. Every quarter or two, task forces look at diversity numbers for the whole company, for business units, and for departments to figure out what needs attention.

After investigating where the problems are—recruitment, career bottlenecks, and so on—task force members come up with solutions, which they then take back to their departments. They notice if their colleagues aren't volunteering to mentor or showing up at recruitment events. Accountability theory suggests that having a task force member in a department will cause managers in it to ask themselves, "Will this look right?" when making hiring and promotion decisions.

Deloitte has seen how powerful social accountability can be. In 1992, Mike Cook, who was then the CEO, decided to try to stanch the hemorrhaging of female associates. Half the company's hires were women, but nearly all of them left before they were anywhere near making partner. As Douglas McCracken, CEO of Deloitte's consulting unit at the time, later recounted in HBR, Cook assembled a high-profile task force that "didn't immediately launch a slew of new organizational policies aimed at outlawing bad behavior" but, rather, relied on transparency to get results.

The task force got each office to monitor the career progress of its women and set its own goals to address local problems. When it became clear that the CEO and other managing partners were closely watching, McCracken wrote, "women started getting their share of premier client assignments and informal mentoring." And unit heads all over the country began getting questions from partners and associates about why things weren't changing faster. An external advisory council issued annual progress reports, and individual managers chose change metrics to add to their own performance ratings. In eight years turnover among women dropped to the same level as turnover among men, and the proportion of female partners increased from 5% to 14%—the highest percentage among the big accounting firms. By 2015, 21% of Deloitte's global partners were women, and in March of that year, Deloitte LLP appointed Cathy Engelbert as its CEO—making her the first woman to head a major accountancy.

Task forces are the trifecta of diversity programs. In addition to promoting accountability, they engage members who might have previously been cool to diversity projects and increase contact among the women, minorities, and white men who participate. They pay off, too: On average, companies that put in diversity task forces see 9% to 30% increases in the representation of white women and of each minority group in management over the next five years.

Once it was clear that top managers were watching, women started to get more premier assignments.

Diversity managers, too, boost inclusion by creating social accountability. To see why, let's go back to the finding of the teacher-in-training experiment, which is supported by many studies: When people know they might have to explain their decisions, they are less likely to act on bias. So simply having a diversity manager who could ask them questions prompts managers to step back and consider everyone who is qualified instead of hiring or promoting the first people who come to mind. Companies that appoint diversity managers see 7% to 18% increases in all underrepresented groups—except Hispanic men—in management in the following five years. Those are the gains after accounting for both effective and ineffective programs they put in place.

Only 20% of medium and large employers have task forces, and just 10% have diversity managers, despite the benefits of both. Diversity managers cost money, but task forces use existing workers, so they're a lot cheaper than some of the things that fail, such as mandatory training.

Leading companies like Bank of America Merrill Lynch, Facebook, and Google have placed big bets on accountability in the past couple of years. Expanding on Deloitte's early example, they're now posting complete diversity numbers for all to see. We should know in a few years if that moves the needle for them.

Strategies for controlling bias—which drive most diversity efforts—have failed spectacularly since they were introduced to promote equal opportunity. Black men have barely gained ground in corporate management since 1985. White women haven't progressed since 2000. It isn't that there aren't enough educated women and minorities out there—both groups have made huge educational gains over the past two generations. The problem is that we can't motivate people by forcing them to get with the program and punishing them if they don't.

Diversity, Equity, and Inclusion

The numbers sum it up. Your organization will become less diverse, not more, if you require managers to go to diversity training, try to regulate their hiring and promotion decisions, and put in a legalistic grievance system.

The very good news is that we know what does work—we just need to do more of it.

VIEWPOINT 3

> "To make inclusion a reality, it's important for organizations to adopt a social model of disability, where disability is viewed as just another difference, like gender or sexuality."

DEI Efforts Aren't Doing Enough to Help Workers with Disabilities

Stephen Friedman

In this viewpoint Stephen Friedman explains that organizations often exclude people with disabilities from their DEI initiatives, and the prevalence of less visible and episodic disabilities further complicates the issue. However, according to research in Canada (where the author is based) 22 percent of Canadians of working age have one or more disabilities, suggesting the urgency of including workers with disabilities in DEI programs. By designing DEI programs to take disabilities into account, businesses have the opportunity to increase their profits and have a broader talent pool. Programs specifically designed for recruiting and mentoring employees with disabilities could have significant benefits for both people with disabilities and their employers. Stephen Friedman is an adjunct professor of organizational studies at the Schulich School of Business at York University in Toronto, Canada.

"Organizations Are Leaving Disabled Workers Behind in Their DEI Efforts—Here's How They Can Do Better," by Stephen Friedman, The Conversation, June 25, 2023, https://theconversation.com/organizations-are-leaving-disabled-workers-behind-in-their-dei-efforts-heres-how-they-can-do-better-207800. Licensed under CC BY-ND 4.0 International.

Diversity, Equity, and Inclusion

As you read, consider the following questions:

1. According to this viewpoint, what percent of Canadian organizations explicitly include disability in their inclusion initiatives?
2. What types of disabilities are considered less visible or episodic?
3. What potential solutions does Friedman offer in this viewpoint?

Diversity, equity and inclusion (DEI) initiatives are becoming increasingly commonplace worldwide. However, when it comes to these efforts, disability is often not given the same level of attention as other factors like gender, ethnicity, culture, race or sexuality. This needs to change.

Only 4 percent of organizations explicitly consider disability in their inclusion initiatives and over 50 percent of global boards and executives report never discussing it. Many organizations leave it out of their DEI efforts altogether.

Despite Canadian legislation prohibiting disability discrimination, disabled people still don't have equal employment opportunities. Over 50 percent of discrimination complaints in Canada involve disability.

Additionally, disabled people are more likely to experience low income, unemployment, underemployment and health-related stress than non-disabled people are.

Not All Disability Is Visible or Constant

The 2017 Canadian Survey on Disability found that over 22 percent of working age Canadians—about 6.2 million — had one or more disabilities. Globally, the number is about 1.3 billion.

The survey also aimed to capture a more accurate picture of disability by including those with invisible and episodic (on-again off-again) disabilities. Examples of these kinds of disabilities include hearing loss, mobility issues, chronic pain, Crohn's, colitis, lupus, multiple sclerosis, addiction and mental health disorders.

Recent data from Statistics Canada shows that the majority of disabilities among Canadians are invisible and/or episodic.

Canadians with episodic and/or invisible disabilities have been experiencing increasing amounts of illegal discrimination in the workplace.

They face a variety of challenges, including feeling as though they can't safely disclose their disability at work. They also experience a lack of organizational support. Over 20 percent of disabled Canadians indicated they were not receiving adequate workplace accommodations in 2017.

Disability Inclusion Is Good for Business

Better-designed DEI efforts can help organizations achieve inclusion outcomes and alleviate stigma that leads to negative employment experiences for people with disabilities.

Organizations' efforts to market their DEI initiatives are a key part of developing an image of inclusivity.

These efforts—successful or not—can bring increased profitability to businesses and improve access to a broader spectrum of talented job applicants.

However, the current reality of overlooking disabled people as potential employees means missed opportunities for everyone involved. This is especially true considering the prevalence of invisible and episodic disabilities.

To achieve real and lasting disability inclusion, organizations should move beyond mostly ineffective approaches that rely solely on special accommodations. These approaches put too much onus on disabled people and too little on business leadership.

What Can Be Done?

There must be a focus on improving leaders' knowledge and understanding regarding how to include disabled people in the workforce.

One interesting approach involves identifying, guiding and mentoring potential leaders who may be overlooked due to their disabilities. One example of this is The Generation Valuable Program, which provides mentorship opportunities to disabled people. The program's first cohort of 75 is currently in progress.

The growth of the gig economy also holds potential for addressing the challenges faced by individuals with invisible and episodic disabilities. In the gig economy, people have the flexibility to manage their work hours and pace of work without having to disclose specific details about their disabilities.

Disabled gig workers could leverage available technologies and services to level the playing field in workplaces. To date, however, the gig economy has not yet had a substantial impact on the underemployment of disabled people. There is a need for much more impactful, profound, systemic change.

Exclusive Solutions Are Not Inclusive

Organizational decision-makers should think more in terms of ability rather than disability, and the untapped talent pool. To make inclusion a reality, it's important for organizations to adopt a social model of disability, where disability is viewed as just another difference, like gender or sexuality.

This stands in contrast to the more common medical model of disability that characterizes disability as a problem that requires accommodation.

A social model of disability involves actively and consistently working towards removing barriers to full participation in employment.

A useful analogy for this approach is a gender-inclusive approach where all bathrooms are designated as gender-neutral, rather than having a single gender-neutral bathroom among a sea of gender-aligned ones.

Ultimately, the responsibility for these types of changes should not rest with disabled people, but with businesses and their leadership.

Combining Social and Commercial Interests

I recently spoke with social entrepreneur, author and Ted Talk speaker, Gil Winch about his outsourcing call center business that employs people with disabilities. It creates a supportive working environment for people with disabilities from recruitment, to training, to physical accommodations.

Winch's business is an example of a social enterprise that combines social good with market-based, commercial interests. With respect to disability, social enterprises aim to develop businesses "where people with a specific disability will have . . . the same capacity" as non-disabled workers.

Winch encourages organizations worldwide to reserve employment for people with disabilities. His reasoning is this: "If we can reserve parking for those with disabilities, why not jobs?"

Given the broad skill set of the world's 1.3 billion disabled people, this idea could help bridge the employment gap.

Why must employment for disabled people be an exception, accommodation or special favor provided by an employer? Why must disabled people feel they have to get permission for flexibility?

Organizations who are serious about DEI must adopt the frame of producing shared value where business and social goods exist side-by-side. Creating real inclusion in employment based on ability is what DEI leadership is all about.

VIEWPOINT 4

> *"The most important factor for whether more deliberate decisions reduce discrimination was a participant's view on affirmative action—the consideration of race in a workforce or student body to ensure that their share of people of color is roughly proportionate to the general public or a local community."*

Racial Bias Is Still a Big Problem in Hiring Practices

Martin Abel

In this viewpoint Martin Abel examines the role racial bias has in hiring practices by looking at how hiring managers view job candidates with Black-sounding names. Abel and his colleague Rulof Burger conducted a study in which people from all 50 U.S. states were asked to participate in a hiring experiment. Many participants had knee-jerk negative reactions toward candidates with names they perceived as Black, considering them less educated, trustworthy, and reliable almost immediately, suggesting significant racial bias. Certain age, gender, racial, and political demographics were more likely to express this bias, but the study showed that rushing to make a decision about candidates had the largest impact on increasing

"Biases Against Black-Sounding First Names Can Lead to Discrimination in Hiring, Especially When Employers Make Decisions in a Hurry—New Research," by Martin Abel, The Conversation, https://theconversation.com/biases-against-black-sounding-first-names-can-lead-to-discrimination-in-hiring-especially-when-employers-make-decisions-in-a-hurry-new-research-208423. Licensed under CC BY-ND 4.0 International.

Does DEI Have a Positive Impact on Marginalized and Minority Groups?

bias. By slowing down the initial assessment of candidates and challenging biased decision-making, racially biased hiring practices can be reduced. Martin Abel is an assistant professor of economics at Bowdoin College in Brunswick, Maine.

As you read, consider the following questions:

1. According to research cited in this viewpoint, which demographic tended to discriminate against candidates with Black-sounding names more?
2. On average, how much time do real-world hiring managers spend reviewing each resume during the initial screening?
3. Which professional fields still have high levels of discriminatory practices?

Because names are among the first things you learn about someone, they can influence first impressions.

That this is particularly true for names associated with Black people came to light in 2004 with the release of a study that found employers seeing identical resumes were 50% more likely to call back an applicant with stereotypical white names like Emily or Greg versus applicants with names like Jamal or Lakisha.

I'm a behavioral economist who researches discrimination in labor markets. In a study based on a hiring experiment I conducted with another economist, Rulof Burger, we found that participants systematically discriminated against job candidates with names they associated with Black people, especially when put under time pressure. We also found that white people who oppose affirmative action discriminated more than other people against job candidates with distinctly Black names, whether or not they had to make rushed decisions.

Detecting Racial Biases

To conduct this study, we recruited 1,500 people from all 50 U.S. states in 2022 to participate in an online experiment on Prolific, a survey platform. The group was nationally representative in terms of race and ethnicity, age and gender.

We first collected data on their beliefs about the race and ethnicity, education, productivity and personality traits of people with six names picked from a pool of 2,400 workers whom we hired in an early stage of our experiment for a transcription task. Data from these individual responses made it possible for us to categorize how they perceived the candidates.

We found that the names of workers perceived as Black, such as Shanice or Terell, were more likely to elicit negative presumptions, such as being less educated, productive, trustworthy and reliable, than people with either white-sounding names, such as Melanie or Adam, or racially ambiguous names, such as Krystal or Jackson.

We were specifically studying discrimination against Black people, so we did not include names in this experiment that are frequently associated with Hispanics or Asians.

Participants were next presented with pairs of names and were told they could earn money for selecting the worker who was more productive in the transcription task. The chance that they would choose job candidates they perceived to be white because of their names was almost twice as high than if they thought the candidates to be Black. This tendency to discriminate against people with Black-sounding names was greatest among men, people over 55, whites and conservatives.

Educational attainment, the level of racial diversity in the participants' ZIP codes or whether they had personally hired anyone before didn't influence their apparent biases.

Rushing Can Cause More Discriminatory Behavior

Most real-world hiring managers spend less than 10 seconds reviewing each resume during the initial screening stage. To keep up that swift pace, they may resort to using mental shortcuts—including racial stereotypes—to assess job applications.

We found that requiring the study participants to select a worker within only 2 seconds led them to be 25% more likely to discriminate against candidates with names they perceived as Black-sounding. Similar patterns of biased decision-making under time pressure have been documented in the context of police shootings and medical decisions.

However, making decisions more slowly is not a panacea.

We found that the most important factor for whether more deliberate decisions reduce discrimination was a participant's view on affirmative action—the consideration of race in a workforce or student body to ensure that their share of people of color is roughly proportionate to the general public or a local community.

White participants who opposed affirmative action were more than twice as likely to select an applicant with a white-sounding name compared with applicants perceived as Black—whether or not they had to make the simulated hiring decision in a hurry.

By contrast, giving white participants who favor affirmative action unlimited time to choose a name from the hiring list reduced discrimination against the job candidates with names they perceived as Black-sounding by almost half. The data showed that this decline had to do with people basing their decision more on their perceptions of a worker's performance, rather than relying on mental shortcuts based on their perceived race.

We assessed the participants' views on affirmative action by doing a survey at the end of this experiment.

Discrimination Hasn't Gone Away

A study published in 2021 suggested that hiring discrimination based on Black-sounding names had declined, although discriminatory practices remained high in some customer-facing lines of work, such as auto sales or retail.

Other research has suggested that once people learn more about someone, the discriminatory influence that a name might

Diversity, Equity, and Inclusion

have begins to fade. Yet, other studies have indicated that racial biases can make the interactions needed for this learning process less likely. For example, racial biases may lead employers to refrain from interviewing—or hiring—a job candidate of color in the first place.

There is ample evidence that people of color face discrimination in many important domains beyond employment, including finding housing or obtaining loans.

Our results suggest that slowing down the initial assessment of applicants can be a first step toward reducing this type of discrimination.

Periodical and Internet Sources Bibliography

The following articles have been selected to supplement the diverse views presented in this chapter.

Kiara Alfonseca and Max Zahn, "How corporate America is slashing DEI workers amid backlash to diversity programs," ABC News, July 7, 2023. https://abcnews.go.com/US/corporate-america-slashing-dei-workers-amid-backlash-diversity/story?id=100477952.

Isla Binnie, "BlackRock's Fink says he's stopped using 'weaponised' term ESG," Reuters, June 26, 2023. https://www.reuters.com/business/environment/blackrocks-fink-says-hes-stopped-using-weaponised-term-esg-2023-06-26.

Marcus Hand, "Shipping company employees want action not words on DEI," Seatrade Maritime, November 28, 2023, https://www.seatrade-maritime.com/ship-operations/shipping-company-employees-want-action-not-words-dei.

Teresa Hopke, "What Companies Are Getting Wrong About DEI," Forbes, January 31, 2024, https://www.forbes.com/sites/teresahopke/2024/01/31/what-companies-are-getting-wrong-about-dei.

Sarah Kessler, "D.E.I. Goes Quiet," the *New York Times*, January 13, 2024. https://www.nytimes.com/2024/01/13/business/dealbook/dei-goes-quiet.html.

Sanja Licina, "How to Use Continuous Listening to Strengthen Your DEI Strategy," Forbes, March 17, 2023. https://www.forbes.com/sites/forbeshumanresourcescouncil/2023/03/17/how-to-use-continuous-listening-to-strengthen-your-dei-strategy/?sh=3a2a888349e7.

Poornima Luthra, "Do Your Global Teams See DEI as an American Issue?" *Harvard Business Review*, March 21, 2022. https://hbr.org/2022/03/do-your-global-teams-see-dei-as-an-american-issue.

Ania G. Masinter, "Overcoming Today's DEI Leadership Challenges," *Harvard Business Review*, September 14, 2023. https://hbr.org/2023/09/overcoming-todays-dei-leadership-challenges.

Jennifer Miller, "Why Some Companies Are Saying 'Diversity and Belonging' Instead of 'Diversity and Inclusion'" the *New York Times*, May 13, 2023. https://www.nytimes.com/2023/05/13/business/diversity-equity-inclusion-belonging.html.

Alex Seitz-Wald and Scott Wong, "Conservatives blame Silicon Valley Bank collapse on 'diversity' and 'woke' issues," NBC News, March 13, 2023. https://www.nbcnews.com/politics/politics-news/go-woke-get-broke-even-financial-crisis-culture-wars-trump-economics-rcna74692.

Ella F. Washington, "The Five Stages of DEI Maturity," *Harvard Business Review*, November-December 2022, https://hbr.org/2022/11/the-five-stages-of-dei-maturity.

CHAPTER 3

| Is DEI Under Attack?

Chapter Preface

A lot of the viewpoints in this chapter focus on how DEI policy has been used in schools, particularly institutions of higher learning like universities and colleges.

In many ways, schools have taken to addressing diversity in a more head-on way than most workplaces, even in the corporate world. Schools often see themselves as idealized spaces, protected by endowments and their nonprofit structure to persist above the fray of capital that dominates the concerns of most businesses. For this reason, they have the latitude to assert their values in a more forceful manner in order to cultivate a particular idea of modern life.

On the other hand, the fact that these institutions are considered to be outside of society but also a representation of it is also the source of so much disagreement in the DEI space. For critics, these programs can represent a kind of top-down censorship that seeks to limit the kinds of discourse these institutions permit. Critics, for instance, see a correlation between diversity programs and a lack of interest in tolerating unpopular or controversial political views. Nowhere does this debate come through as vividly as in arguments over so-called diversity statements, which a number of schools have started to request employees create.

While higher education serves as the venue for many of the debates around whether DEI is being unfairly maligned or rightfully criticized, some of the viewpoints in this chapter also focus on criticisms of DEI in the workplace. The viewpoints in this chapter take a number of such stands from both sides of the growing political divide.

VIEWPOINT 1

> "The challenges come as companies, faced with an uncertain economy, have already been laying off large numbers of people, including many only recently hired to implement their diversity, equity and inclusion (DEI) strategies."

Cutbacks and Legal Attacks Threaten DEI Initiatives

Andrea Hsu

In this viewpoint, Andrea Hsu writes about some of the major criticisms that have emerged in recent years from conservative critics of DEI. According to Hsu, recent court rulings have leaned against giving organizations the power to use strategies like affirmative action, a major part of diversity policy. The viewpoint presents the idea that these issues are part of a reactionary response to the most recent wave of diversity policy. Hsu warns that events like these could discourage corporations from pursuing DEI initiatives, especially those that weren't enthusiastic about them to begin with. This is bad news for people who work in the DEI industry, who tell Hsu that they are having trouble staying employed. Hsu is a labor and workplace reporter at NPR and has been working at the news nonprofit since 2002.

© 2023 National Public Radio, Inc. NPR news report titled "Corporate DEI initiatives are facing cutbacks and legal attacks" by Andrea Hsu was originally published on npr.org on August 19, 2023, and is used with the permission of NPR. Any unauthorized duplication is strictly prohibited.

Diversity, Equity, and Inclusion

As you read, consider the following questions:
1. Why did the Supreme Court reject the use of race-conscious admissions in higher education?
2. What is this viewpoint's take on the future of affirmative action?
3. What are some of the criticisms of corporate diversity, equity, and inclusion efforts that this viewpoint mentions?

Just three years after the murder of George Floyd in Minneapolis set off a torrent of hiring of chief diversity officers and other such roles, companies are coming under attack from conservative legal activists who argue that their DEI policies and programs constitute racial discrimination.

The challenges come as companies, faced with an uncertain economy, have already been laying off large numbers of people, including many only recently hired to implement their diversity, equity and inclusion (DEI) strategies.

The one-two punch has legal experts split on what's ahead for these efforts, while longtime diversity advocates argue that companies should take these setbacks as an opportunity to reset.

"We cannot place the reasoning for it on something as subjective as the right thing to do. It has to be the smart thing to do," says Janet Stovall, global head of diversity, equity and inclusion for the NeuroLeadership Institute, a consulting firm focused on culture and leadership.

A Surge in Hiring, Followed by Dramatic Cuts

In the corporate DEI world, Catalina Colman's story is a familiar one.

In 2020, she was working at a small tech company as a human resources generalist, handling tasks such as employee onboardings and exits.

She had already been thinking about how to help the company grow in a more diverse and equitable way, when in May of that year, George Floyd was murdered. Suddenly, everything accelerated.

"We recognized we just needed to move quickly, and we needed to start implementing things fast," says Colman.

The racial reckoning unfolding across the country unleashed demands for change. Companies scrambled to respond to the moment. According to the jobs site Indeed, job postings with DEI in the title jumped 92% from July 2020 to July 2021.

But the deceleration has also come quickly. Economic pressures have led companies to pull back, cutting DEI jobs including Colman's alongside other human resources roles. Since last July, Indeed has seen DEI job postings drop by 38%.

And then in June, in another blow to diversity advocates, the Supreme Court rejected the use of race-conscious admissions in higher education, setting off predictions that corporate policies around diversity will soon meet the same fate.

Predictions of What's Next for Corporate DEI

To be clear, the court's decision applies to affirmative action at colleges and universities, not employer efforts to foster diversity in the workplace.

In a statement issued after the ruling, Charlotte Burrows, chair of the Equal Employment Opportunity Commission, wrote, "It remains lawful for employers to implement diversity, equity, inclusion, and accessibility programs that seek to ensure workers of all backgrounds are afforded equal opportunity in the workplace."

But in a Bloomberg opinion piece, Harvard Law professor Noah Feldman cited Justice Neil Gorsuch's concurring opinion, in which "he made it crystal clear that in his view, the court's rule that an educational institution 'may never discriminate based on race' now applies with equal force to employers."

Feldman told NPR the writing is on the wall.

"There's a high probability, a very high probability, that a majority of this current Supreme Court will say the exact same thing," he said in an interview last month.

But other attorneys say such assumptions are premature. Bonnie Levine, founder of the law firm Verse Legal, points out that a day after the affirmative action decision, the Supreme Court ruled that a Christian wedding website designer could refuse to work with same-sex couples.

"The Supreme Court has been very clear about not wanting to infringe on the rights of private parties," says Levine.

Regardless, conservative activists are already waging a new fight.

In early August, Edward Blum, the strategist behind the affirmative action case, filed a lawsuit against the venture capital group Fearless Fund over grants it awards to Black female entrepreneurs. Blum argues that the program amounts to "express and intentional racial discrimination in the making of contracts," according to the lawsuit.

Former Trump adviser Stephen Miller has also been busy, asking the EEOC to investigate hiring practices aimed at increasing minority representation at a long list of companies including Kellogg's, Hershey and Alaska Airlines.

"They are bringing these cases to make law. That's why they're bringing them," says Levine.

A Moment to Get Out or Double Down

Even before this year, corporate diversity, equity and inclusion efforts have come under harsh criticism, including that they're expensive, performative, even a source of division themselves.

At companies where DEI was never a priority, this may be a moment to get out.

"It makes sense that you wouldn't want to just jump into something that is going to be more complicated if you don't feel like you have to," says consultant Stovall.

But for clients who are in it for the long haul, Stovall is doubling down on advice she's always given: Focus on the rationale. Make the business case for bringing on a diversity of backgrounds and experiences.

"Every organization has basically only three goals: make money, save money, achieve a vision," she says. "If you can tie DEI directly to one of those goals, it gets a little bit harder for even those who want to destroy it to argue that they should."

For Catalina Colman, trying to find another DEI job after her layoff in April was disheartening. Positions she applied for were eliminated midway through the interview process.

This summer, she decided to put herself out there as an independent consultant. She's banking on companies wanting to continue the work they started, recognizing a business imperative.

"Consumers, users are still going to want—at the end of the day—diversity to be a key pillar for an organization," she says.

VIEWPOINT 2

> "Addressing this opposition requires recognizing the systemic issues that hinder equal opportunity and fostering a dialogue that emphasizes the benefits of diverse perspectives."

What Causes Resistance to DEI Initiatives?

Marcus Bright

In this viewpoint, Marcus Bright writes about regulations aimed at restricting the use of state and federal funds for DEI programs that were signed into law by Florida Governor Ron DeSantis in May 2023. Bright writes that this law is just one example of the growing and vigorous resistance to initiatives aimed at the furtherance of diversity, equity, and inclusion policy. He has organized the viewpoint around three different criticisms that these legislative efforts have focused on, which appear to be part of a larger culture war. Marcus Bright is a writer for a website called Diverse, which focuses on policy in the higher education space.

As you read, consider the following questions:

1. Why does this viewpoint argue that the mass marketing of Black celebrities has inadvertently contributed to the opposition towards DEI initiatives?

"Unpacking the Pillars of Resistance Against DEI Initiatives" by Marcus Bright. Cox Matthews and Associates, Inc., January 7, 2024. Reprinted with permission. From Diverse Issues in Higher Education, DiverseEducation.com

2. What's the connection between immigration issues and DEI policy?
3. According to Bright, what do the cultural issues underpinning DEI criticisms have to do with the presidency of Donald Trump?

The political landscape in Florida has recently witnessed some significant developments that pose a serious challenge to efforts aimed at promoting diversity, equity, and inclusion (DEI) initiatives at public colleges and universities.

On November 8, 2023, the Florida Board of Governors put forth regulations aimed at restricting the use of state and federal funds for DEI programs. This decision aligns with the bill signed into law by Governor Ron DeSantis in May 2023. The Board of Governors is expected to have a final vote on adopting the regulations at their meeting on January 24, 2024.

Among the language of the draft regulations that outlines what will be prohibited is as follows: "a state university or state university direct-support organization advocates for DEI when it engages in a program, policy or activity that:

(a) Advantages or disadvantages, or attempts to advantage or disadvantage an individual or group on the basis of color, sex, national origin, gender identity, or sexual orientation, to equalize or increase outcomes, participation or representation as compared to other individuals or groups;

or

(b) Promotes the position that a group or an individual's action is inherently, unconsciously, or implicitly biased on the basis of color, sex, national origin, gender identity, or sexual orientation."

By implementing policies such as these that restrict DEI initiatives, Florida is effectively cementing advantages gained through a history of discrimination. The implications of such actions extend far beyond the borders of Florida, as other states may be influenced by this precedent, hindering their own advancements in DEI initiatives.

This is but one example of a growing and vigorous resistance to initiatives aimed at the furtherance of diversity, equity, and inclusion. I have listed some of the pillars of resistance against DEI programs below:

Pillar of Resistance #1—Limited Opportunity "Lottery" System of Qualified Applicants

In numerous industries, there exists an implicit lottery system where a small number of highly coveted positions are available, leading to intense competition among applicants. Regardless of qualifications or capabilities, individuals may find themselves overlooked simply due to the scarcity of available slots. This situation is not reflective of one's ability to adequately fulfill different roles but rather a systemic issue perpetuated by a lack of sufficient opportunities.

The limited number of highly desirable jobs intensifies misperceptions surrounding DEI initiatives. Some individuals mistakenly believe that the push for diversity aims to lower standards or compromise quality in hiring and promotion processes. This misunderstanding fuels opposition, as critics argue that merit should be the sole determinant rather than considering factors such as race, gender, or ethnicity.

Limited opportunities are often exacerbated by existing institutional barriers and ingrained practices within industries. These barriers perpetuate inequality by favoring traditional candidate profiles and excluding individuals from underrepresented groups. The resistance to change stems from a fear of disrupting the status quo, perpetuating opposition to DEI initiatives that seek to dismantle these barriers.

Addressing this opposition requires recognizing the systemic issues that hinder equal opportunity and fostering a dialogue that emphasizes the benefits of diverse perspectives and inclusivity at higher education institutions and in the workforce.

Pillar #2—The Mass Marketing of Celebrity Lifestyles

The mass marketing of celebrities, particularly Black celebrities, has inadvertently contributed to the opposition towards DEI initiatives. Attorney Antonio Moore referred to this concept as the "Decadent Veil" in a 2014 *Huffington Post* article. Moore wrote in reference to the concept that "despite a large section of the 14 million Black households drowning in poverty and debt, the stories of a few are told as if they represent those of millions, not thousands. It is this new veil of economics that has allowed for a broad swath of America to become not just desensitized to Black poverty, but also hypnotized by Black celebrity. How could we not? Our channels from ESPN to VH1 are filled with presentations of Black Americans being paid a king's ransom to entertain. As Black celebrity has been shown to millions of people, millions of times, the story of real lives has also been lost, and with it the engine that thrust forward the demand for social justice by the masses."

By focusing on the success stories of a select few, the true extent of racial inequality is obscured behind the glamour and glitz of celebrity lifestyles. This creates an illusion that corrective justice and addressing disparate opportunities are no longer necessary, hindering progress in DEI efforts.

Pillar #3—The Tying Together of Immigration and Opposition to DEI Initiatives

The intertwining of immigration with DEI has provided ammunition for those looking to undermine how many DEI initiatives that include people who recently arrived in the United States from other counties, leading to a growing public opinion narrative against DEI and even incentivizing lawmakers to advance policies aimed at dismantling it.

The 2016 presidential election saw Donald Trump successfully harness a forceful and aggressive anti-immigration fervor to propel him into the White House. This same tone and tenor have proven politically potent in the current 2024 presidential election race.

Consequently, associating opposition to DEI with being against an open borders type of immigration policy can wield considerable political influence among certain constituencies.

Another critique related to immigration is centered around the influx of individuals on H1-B visas, who are then classified as "minorities" to fulfill diversity metrics. This critique argues that this use of "DEI" takes away opportunities for American citizens more broadly and, more specifically, other native-born people of color who have historically experienced legalized oppression and marginalization in America.

The blending of immigration concerns with opposition to DEI initiatives has cultivated a narrative that undermines the goals of diversity, equity, and inclusion. It is crucial to recognize and address these concerns while advocating for the importance of DEI initiatives. By disentangling the immigration discourse from the conversation around diversity, equity, and inclusion, we can foster a more nuanced understanding of the benefits that diverse perspectives and backgrounds bring to our society as a whole.

Conclusion

It is crucial to recognize the wider implications of the dismantling of DEI initiatives at Florida public colleges and universities. The advancement of efforts to dismantle DEI raises concerns not only about the ability of higher education institutions to promote inclusivity, but also threatens other industries as it pertains to having mechanisms with the capacity to address historical inequalities faced by marginalized groups.

To truly understand the impact of policies like these, we must acknowledge the deep-seated historical context of discrimination and its far-reaching consequences. The racial wealth gaps we see today are not just the result of individual choices or mere happenstance; they are the product of a complex web of factors. Federal Housing Administration policies, slavery, Jim Crow laws, employment discrimination, and the denial of access to capital, among other systemic injustices, have contributed to the enduring disparities that we currently see.

Imagine starting a 26-mile marathon with a 13-mile disadvantage and then having policies enacted that prevent any effort to address or even study how this head start was gained. History matters today because the advantages accumulated from generations of past discrimination continue to manifest as intergenerational transfers of wealth.

These transfers subsidize college costs, enable car purchases, cover private school payments, support credit card bills, pay medical expenses, provide business start-up capital, facilitate homeownership, and fund other significant purchases. The vast disparity in wealth-building opportunities perpetuates economic inequality and limits the upward mobility of marginalized communities.

By understanding the pillars of resistance against DEI programs, we can effectively challenge the attacks on diversity, equity, and inclusion. It is crucial to recognize the deep-seated historical context of discrimination and its far-reaching consequences to work towards a more inclusive and just society for all.

VIEWPOINT 3

> "The size of a university's DEI bureaucracy is, however, strongly correlated with how students feel about allowing controversial conservative speakers on campus."

Against the DEI Industry

Kevin Wallsten

In this viewpoint Kevin Wallsten argues that DEI programs employ cadres of bureaucrats who fail to assimilate into institutional contexts such as universities, which are supposed to prioritize truth-seeking and free expression. According to Wallsten, there's a connection between the rise of DEI policies at colleges and what critics are calling a free speech crisis on college campuses. In fact, he argues that there is a direct connection between the measure of a university's DEI initiative and illiberal attitudes toward speech among students. Most potently, he claims to have discovered a strong connection between the number of DEI employees at a school with how students claim to feel about allowing certain controversial conservative speakers on campuses. Kevin Wallsten is a professor of political science at California State University, Long Beach.

"Is DEI Causing the 'Crisis of Free Speech' on Campus?" by Kevin Wallsten. Heterodox Academy, December 6, 2023. Reprinted with permission.

As you read, consider the following questions:

1. According to this viewpoint, why is it difficult to assimilate DEI principles and personnel into an institutional context?
2. What does this viewpoint say are the potential trade-offs between DEI and free expression?
3. In what way does this viewpoint connect DEI programs with how liberal speakers and conservative speakers are treated at universities?

Universities are making increasingly expansive commitments to diversity, equity, and inclusion (DEI). Effectuating these commitments has necessitated the hiring of a vast new cadre of costly bureaucrats dedicated to advancing DEI at every level of the university. To take just one example, the Equity & Inclusion division at the University of California, Berkeley grew from 110 employees in 2017 to 170 in 2022. In total, Berkeley now spends more than $25 million each year on DEI-related activities.

It is often unclear, however, how DEI principles and the personnel required to implement them are supposed to assimilate into an institutional context that also prioritizes truth-seeking and free expression. Some DEI offices are attempting to harmonize DEI and free speech imperatives by explicitly highlighting areas of conflict and consonance in their public-facing communications. For instance, the UCLA's Office of Equity, Diversity and Inclusion's website explains that although "freedom of expression and freedom of inquiry form bedrock principles central to our mission to pursue knowledge and understanding... freedom of speech is... limited by other rights and values, such as equality."

Yet other universities are more reticent about potential trade-offs between DEI and free expression. This reticence, coupled with a relentless stream of high-profile controversies centered around DEI-based objections to campus speech, has led many to conclude that DEI and free expression are incompatible. In a widely circulated Wall Street Journal op-ed titled "How 'Diversity' Turned Tyrannical," for example, Lawrence Krauss argued that DEI stifles free expression by creating "a climate of pervasive fear on campus." As Krauss puts it, "The DEI monomania has contributed to the crisis of free speech on campus."

These sentiments are fueling a fierce backlash against university DEI initiatives. According to one recent count, more than 30 state governments are taking steps to regulate, reform, or abolish DEI programs, with most justifying their efforts on free speech grounds. But there's no solid evidence—only speculation and anecdotes—guiding the movement to "end DEI." To date, there have been no systematic, empirical studies assessing the relationship between DEI initiatives and campus speech climates.

Correctly diagnosing the effects of DEI programs is a necessary condition for devising effective and appropriately targeted solutions to the campus "free speech crisis." The analyses below are an initial attempt to provide such a diagnosis. Combining a novel measure of a university's DEI bureaucracy with university-level survey data, I show that universities with larger DEI bureaucracies are less tolerant of conservative speakers and more supportive of disruptive actions to prevent campus speech. While the magnitude of DEI's negative effects on campus expression are not large enough to validate the policy prescriptions endorsed by DEI's harshest critics, the fact that larger DEI bureaucracies are correlated with more illiberal student attitudes toward speech should invite reflection about whether DEI bureaucracies are approaching their work in a way that most effectively promotes the indispensable values of diversity, equity, and inclusion.

Measuring University DEI Bureaucracies

There is no centralized database archiving information about the size of university DEI programs. The only cross-campus study of DEI bureaucracies to date was produced by Jay Greene and James Paul for the Heritage Foundation. Their study, summarized in a report titled "Diversity University: DEI Bloat in the Academy," examined 65 universities from the "Power Five" athletic conferences: the Atlantic Coast Conference, the Big 10, the Big 12, the PAC 12, and the Southeastern Conference.

To identify the number of DEI employees at each of these schools, Greene and Paul conducted keyword searches of university websites. Specifically, they searched for terms such as "diversity," "Multicultural Affairs," "Women's Center," and "LGBTQ Center." Staff and interns identified through these searches were added to their university's count of DEI personnel.

The 65 schools Greene and Paul selected were "mainstream institutions." Their data cannot be used, therefore, to assess the impact of DEI bureaucracies at small liberal arts colleges or highly selective, elite universities. The latter limitation is particularly troubling given that highly selective, elite universities produce a disproportionate share of future leaders and serve as role models for lower-ranked universities.

For these reasons, I expanded on Greene and Paul's work by applying their search-based method to a larger group of universities. Specifically, I recorded the number of DEI personnel at the top 20 ranked liberal arts colleges and the top 50 ranked "national universities," according to *US News & World Report*'s 2022 rankings. When combined with the 65 schools in Greene and Paul's report, this approach produced a sample of 109 universities.

The resulting data shows wide variation in the number of DEI employees across universities, with 15 schools that have fewer than one DEI employee for every 1,000 undergraduates (e.g., Baylor University, Auburn University, University of Alabama, University of Florida, West Virginia University) and 17 schools that have more than six DEI employees for every 1,000 undergraduates (e.g., Harvard University, Stanford University, Georgetown University, Duke University, Williams College). Generally speaking, however, private universities have more DEI employees than public universities, and highly ranked universities tend to have more DEI employees than lower-ranked universities.

The Relationship Between DEI and Intolerance of Controversial Speakers

In 2023 the Foundation for Individual Rights and Expression (FIRE) conducted a nationwide survey of more than 55,000 students at 254 universities. FIRE's survey asked students a series of questions to assess how tolerant they were of controversial speakers. Specifically, students were asked whether three speakers who had previously espoused the following controversial liberal ideas should be allowed on campus:

- The Second Amendment should be repealed so that guns can be confiscated.
- Structural racism maintains inequality by protecting white privilege.
- Religious liberty is used as an excuse to discriminate against gays and lesbians.

Students were also asked whether three speakers who had previously espoused the following controversial conservative ideas should be allowed on campus:

- Abortion should be completely illegal.
- Transgender people have a mental disorder.
- Black Lives Matter is a hate group.

Only two schools in the FIRE survey—Hillsdale College and Liberty University—were more intolerant of liberal speakers than of conservative speakers. Further, the differences in tolerance for liberal and conservative speakers at most universities were often quite large, with intolerance averaging 34.6% for liberal speakers and 66.8% for conservative speakers.

In order to identify the impact of DEI bureaucracies on political tolerance, I conducted a series of OLS regression models predicting university-level tolerance for controversial liberal and conservative speakers. In addition to the aforementioned measure of the size of a university's DEI bureaucracy, these models also included a number of variables intended to capture other influences on a university's speech climate; namely, the amount of diversity in the university's student population (racial, ethnic, gender and political/viewpoint), the permissiveness of the university's "speech codes," and whether the university is a public or private institution.

The size of a university's DEI bureaucracy is not significantly correlated with more (or less) intolerance of any of the controversial liberal speakers. The estimated percentage of students opposed to allowing each of the three liberal speakers mentioned in the FIRE survey on campus is roughly the same at universities with small and large DEI bureaucracies. In other words, having more DEI employees on a campus does not influence how tolerant students are of controversial liberal speakers.

The size of a university's DEI bureaucracy is, however, strongly correlated with how students feel about allowing controversial conservative speakers on campus. Universities with a larger number of DEI employees also have a larger percentage of students who say that controversial conservative speakers "probably" or "definitely" should not be allowed to speak on campus. For example, support for preventing a speaker who once said "Black Lives Matter is a hate group" is predicted to jump from 66% at universities with the smallest DEI bureaucracies to nearly 80% at universities with the largest DEI bureaucracies.

The Relationship Between DEI and Support for Disruptive Action

FIRE's survey also asked students about the acceptability of "shouting down a speaker to prevent them from speaking on campus," "blocking other students from attending a campus speech," and "using violence to stop a campus speech." Once again, there was tremendous variation across universities. Students at Grinnell College, for example, were five times more likely than students at Hillsdale College to say that it is "rarely," "sometimes," or "always" acceptable to shout down a speaker to prevent them from speaking on campus. Similarly, Oberlin College students were five times more likely than Brigham Young University students to say that there are circumstances in which it is acceptable to use "violence to stop a campus speech."

Even after controlling for the other variables discussed above, the size of a university's DEI bureaucracy is significantly and positively correlated with student support for disruptive action. To be more exact, compared with universities with the smallest DEI bureaucracies, universities with the largest DEI bureaucracies are predicted to have student populations that are 19% more supportive of shout-downs, 10% more supportive of blockades, and 12% more supportive of violence.

Conclusion

There's congealing conventional wisdom among critics of higher education that DEI bureaucracies are "cancers that stifle free speech." These critics assume a zero-sum relationship between diversity, equity, and inclusion and free expression. Empirically speaking, these assumptions are not completely unwarranted. Larger DEI bureaucracies are correlated with reduced tolerance of conservative speakers and increased support for disruptive action. And, there's no evidence in the data analyzed here that having more DEI employees fosters healthier speech climates on college campuses.

None of this should be taken, however, as an endorsement of recent calls to "end DEI." DEI bureaucracies are not exclusively (or primarily) designed to serve as caretakers of a university's speech environment, and they may produce a host of benefits beyond free speech that universities now deem central to fulfilling their core missions. What's more, the analyses presented above are limited in that they rely on imperfect data (e.g., the measure of DEI personnel is imprecise and was collected for an unrepresentative sample of only 110 universities, the measure of student attitudes was derived from a single year of survey data, the regression models may have left out important but unmeasured influences on campus speech climates, etc.) and cannot be used to definitively identify the direction of causality (i.e., they cannot tell us whether larger

DEI bureaucracies produce more censorious students or more censorious students produce larger DEI bureaucracies). Even taking the findings at face value, the impact of DEI bureaucracies is not large enough to believe that eliminating them would single-handedly solve the campus "free speech crisis." Illiberal inclinations among college students clearly have deeper origins.

Instead, these findings should simply serve as an invitation to begin the process of reimagining DEI so that it might function in ways that are less antagonistic to the university's "truth-seeking" telos.

VIEWPOINT 4

> *"This doesn't mean that every person who opposes DEI training is racist. But it does mean that people with the most negative racial attitudes are, on average, most opposed to DEI training."*

Attacks on DEI Are Rooted in Racism

Tatishe Nteta, Adam Eichen, Douglas Rice, Jesse Rhodes, and Justin H. Gross

In this viewpoint Tatishe Nteta, Adam Eichen, Douglas Rice, Jesse Rhodes, and Justin H. Gross discuss the findings of a poll they conducted on the connection between racial attitudes and support for DEI programs. The goal of their study was to discover if opposition to DEI programs is rooted in racism. The authors found that people who believed that racism did not exist or were not bothered by it were more likely to disapprove of DEI programs. While not everyone who opposes DEI is racist, the authors argue that the data suggests that those who do oppose it are more likely to be racist. Tatishe Nteta is a provost professor of political science and director of the UMass Poll at the University of Massachusetts, Amherst, where Douglas Rice is an associate professor of political science and legal studies, Jesse Rhodes is an associate professor of political science, Justin H. Gross is an associate professor of political science and computational social

"Yes, Efforts to Eliminate DEI Programs Are Rooted in Racism" by Tatishe Nteta, Adam Eichen, Douglas Rice, Jesse Rhodes, and Justin H. Gross, The Conversation, April 5, 2024, https://theconversation.com/yes-efforts-to-eliminate-dei-programs-are-rooted-in-racism-227028. Licensed under CC BY-ND 4.0 International

science, and Adam Eichen was a PhD student in political science at the time this viewpoint was published.

As you read, consider the following questions:
1. At the time this viewpoint was published in 2024, which states had passed anti-DEI legislation?
2. Which professions do the majority of Americans believe should receive DEI training?
3. What negative racial attitudes were considered in the survey?

Right-wing activists who have long criticized liberalism and "wokeness" in higher education and helped force the resignation of Claudine Gay, Harvard University's first African American president, have now set their sights on ending the diversity, equity and inclusion, or DEI, programs that these activists claim helped place figures like Gay in her job in the first place.

Christopher Rufo, the conservative activist who played a pivotal role in forcing Gay's resignation, stated this view bluntly on X—formerly known as Twitter—following Gay's ouster: "Today, we celebrate victory. Tomorrow, we get back to the fight. We must not stop until we have abolished DEI ideology from every institution in America."

The DEI initiatives and programs at the center of these controversies aim to help organizations identify and more effectively tackle disparities or inequities in their organizations.

In the past year, a number of states have begun to dismantle their DEI programs. Alabama, Utah, Texas and Florida have all passed and signed into law anti-DEI legislation ranging from prohibiting diversity training to terminating all positions associated with DEI efforts. Florida lawmakers have restricted the teaching of what they call racially "divisive"

Diversity, Equity, and Inclusion

subject matter in public schools, colleges and universities. Legislatures in more than two dozen additional states are considering similar measures.

Critics of these measures say they are racist. DEI opponents are quick to deny this.

Is opposition to DEI programs unrelated to racism? Or does racism play an important role in opposition to DEI programs?

We are survey researchers who study how racial attitudes affect Americans' attitudes toward public policies. In a recent poll, we investigated what, if any, influence racism may have on public opinion toward DEI programs.

Attacks on DEI

Just when you thought you'd seen it all, something else comes out of the water that shakes everything up. Since the death of George Floyd, we have seen a big push for diversity, equity, and inclusion (DEI). I have seen this in different forms of advertisement, businesses, and even on television shows. The thing I like most about DEI is that it does give certain ethnic groups opportunities that they may not have had before. DEI put pressure on different companies, businesses, schools, colleges, even Hollywood, etc., to be diverse and inclusive to all.

We live in a diverse world, so why not have different entities that reflect that. However, there are a few individuals who don't agree with this notion. Not too long ago, Senate Bill 17 was approved in a 19 to 12 vote. This bill will require universities and colleges to end their DEI programs and initiatives. It would also ban schools from any DEI training for employees, or asking any DEI-related questions in interviews, etc. Of course, legislation has also tied this to funding and schools can be penalized if they don't comply.

If everything was equitable in our world, we wouldn't have had a need for DEI in the first place. Those that are against DEI claim that it would turn back the hands of time to discrimination and make certain

Implausible Claims About DEI

Utah Gov. Spencer Cox defended anti-DEI measures in his state by characterizing them as reaffirming the ideal of colorblindness in American society.

"We used to aspire toward the dream of Martin Luther King Jr. of a future where our children 'will not be judged by the color of their skin, but by the content of their character,'" he said. "Now, Americans are accused of systemic racism for quoting these same immortal words of Dr. King. Up is down."

But statements by other conservative politicians and commentators seem more transparently racist.

> ethnic groups not feel welcome. Well, wasn't that the reason why DEI was created? DEI was created so all people could feel included and valued. When we think of DEI, some may automatically assume race. However, DEI also includes gender, political affiliation, social status, sexual orientation, etc. Now legislation wants to take that away. All of this is very contradictory for me. Because getting rid of DEI programs does take us back. It eliminates any little progress we have made in creating an inclusive world for all.
>
> We will never forget the death of George Floyd as I believe his death nationally showcased the state of America when it comes to race, justice, freedom, exclusion, hatred, and so much more. Now it just seems as if DEI was just a check off and not even a sincere push for equity across the board. I believe that DEI should remain in schools. It has done a lot of good and has opened doors for many who may have been overlooked because of their background.
>
> When will we start seeing people for just people? When will we stop making everything political and just do the right thing? As Jacqueline Woods said, "Diversity is about all of us having to figure out how to walk through this world together."
>
> "Diversity, Equity, Inclusion are Under Attack" by Chelsea Davis-Bibb, African American News & Issues, May 6, 2023.

Diversity, Equity, and Inclusion

Following the deadly accident that destroyed the Francis Scott Key Bridge in Baltimore, several Republican elected officials and candidates claimed—implausibly—that DEI policies were responsible. One conservative commentator reposted video footage of a news conference on the tragedy held by Baltimore Mayor Brandon Scott, who is Black, with the comment, "This is Baltimore's DEI mayor commenting on the collapsed Francis Scott Key Bridge. It's going to get so, so much worse. Prepare accordingly."

In our January 2024 survey of a nationally representative sample of 1,064 U.S. adults, we sought to identify what influence racism may have on public opinion about DEI programs. We asked respondents, "From the following list, please indicate if you believe the indicated professionals and/or members of institutions should or should not receive Diversity, Equity, and Inclusion (DEI) training."

The list included medical professionals, teachers, police officers, members of the U.S. armed forces, public sector employees and private sector employees.

Next, we assessed respondents' racial attitudes with questions that measure their acknowledgment of the existence of racism in the U.S. and their emotional reaction to the problem of racism in the nation. We also asked respondents about their partisan identity, ideological affiliation and demographic characteristics.

'Huge' Impact on Support for DEI

We found that a strong majority of Americans support DEI training for each of the professions we listed in the survey. On average, 7 in 10 Americans support DEI training for medical professionals, teachers, police officers, members of the U.S. armed forces and public employees, while 65% of Americans support this training for private sector employees.

However, among Americans with negative racial attitudes—which is a phrase used by scholars of public opinion to characterize respondents who hold prejudicial, stereotypical or racist views of people of color—support for DEI training was much lower.

On average, only 46% of Americans who believe that racial problems are rare support DEI training; 45% of those who are not angry that racism exists support DEI training, and 38% of those who do not believe that white people have advantages because of their skin color support DEI training programs.

Next, we summed up interviewees' responses across questions to create an overall measure of support for DEI training and analyzed how negative racial attitudes affect support for DEI. We did this while taking into account characteristics such as gender identity, age, education, income, race, political party identification and ideology.

After taking these characteristics into account, we found that the effect of negative racial attitudes on support for DEI programs was huge. Support for DEI programs was 73 percentage points lower among individuals with the most negative racial attitudes compared to those with the most positive attitudes.

This doesn't mean that every person who opposes DEI training is racist. But it does mean that people with the most negative racial attitudes are, on average, most opposed to DEI training.

Many Americans understandably wish that the nation has achieved Martin Luther King Jr.'s dream of a "colorblind" society. But the troubling connection between racism and opposition to DEI programs highlights that there is still work to be done until the nation's citizens are truly judged by the content of their character and not the color of their skin.

VIEWPOINT

> "Rationally, since white students do not see diversity missing, they do not regard its lack as a problem. It makes no sense to spend extra university efforts on increasing diversity since diversity already proliferates across campus."

Universities that Advertise Diversity Increase Racism

Arthur Scarritt

In this viewpoint Arthur Scarritt discusses how the tendency of universities to advertise their diversity in order to raise money ends up causing white students to become more racist and BIPOC students to feel deceived. By making students believe that diversity is already a part of the campus experience at these universities, they come to understand diversity as any kind of differences, including trivial, meaningless ones. Consequently, they come to believe that centering social justice around race is unfair. They believe that the treatment of students should be "colorblind," including the distribution of scholarships and financial aid, without taking into account that BIPOC students are disproportionately impacted by high tuition rates. Scarritt argues that effective diversity initiatives do exist, but that superficial ones do more harm than good. Dr. Arthur Scarritt a professor and chair of the department of sociology at Boise State University in Idaho.

"How Commercializing Diversity Promotes Racism," by Dr. Arthur Scarritt, Spark: Elevating Scholarship on Social Issues, 2021. Reprinted with permission.

As you read, considering the following questions:

1. How did BIPOC students react in response to advertising of diversity? How did responses from white students differ?
2. What is "colorblind racism"?
3. What initiatives and ideas about diversity does Scarritt believe could actually be beneficial?

Universities raising money by advertising diversity actually increase racism among white students. Universities across the U.S., like mine, make official statements that they are "actively committed to diversity and inclusivity, a stance in alignment with our Statement of Shared Values." Such proclamations are mostly aspirational, saying the university would certainly like more diversity and is not going to take active measures to stop it.

At the same time, universities use diversity as advertising to attract students, with web pages, glossy printed materials, and colorful posters disproportionately featuring people of color. But using diversity as advertising makes aspirational statements non-aspirational like assessments of existing conditions. As with other forms of advertising, universities are trying to attract students based on what the university supposedly is: "Come to us to get this." Both white and BIPOC students take the university at its word—that it actively supports diversity.

Most BIPOC students feel deceived when they find this is not true. We discovered this as part of a larger project for which we have been conducting open-ended interviews with students about their takes on higher education, including race and diversity. Most white students, however, reacted very differently from their BIPOC peers. And this is what makes advertising so problematic in higher education. Students must trust that universities have their best interests at heart. But advertising is "conscious and intelligent manipulation," as Edward Bernays famously put it, convincing through using exaggerated, enticing, and even false representations.

Put in the context of diversity, we found that white students trusted the university's uncritical advertising of diversity—that diversity already flourished at the university. Like other scholars, we found students seeing diversity as uncritically good: "Diversity is wonderful," explained one typical white student. More to the point, since the university said diversity existed across campus, white students read diversity into almost every aspect of college life. As one young woman explained diversity to us:

> I know a lot of people, more so with girls, flock to the education building a little bit, some of them even more to [a different building] because it has food and we're girls, most of us are hungry. . . . I know the library is very diverse in that way, you can tell who the rowdier groups are because they stay on the first or second floor and more of us study-oriented or shy, lonely people, or if you just study alone they go up to the third or fourth floor. But you see just who cares more about academics or if you are a group you stay on the first floor.

Herein anything variable on campus becomes diversity, including buildings or floors on buildings. Another student gives even broader examples:

> . . . different everything, there is a lot of different types of candies, my backpack is diverse, there are a lot of different materials and things in it. It also, it's not, I don't think I have ever seen someone with the same backpack as me.

As another student summed it up, diversity is "the entire world! All planet Earth." That is, everything is part of diversity, and nothing is not a part of diversity. The concept becomes a meaningless collection of trivial differences. With the backpack example, diversity is both the different elements that make up a product—embodying diversity in and of itself and also how these differences add up to distinction even though almost everyone has a backpack. Diversity becomes an unavoidable, constantly changing aspect of everyday life. Everyone experiences it because everyone does different things at different times. It is everywhere and means almost nothing. And the university indirectly supports this perspective, by explaining that "Diversity is the variety of intersecting identities that make individuals unique"—everyone is diverse because everything contributes to diversity.

What happens to race under such conditions? Rationally, since white students do not see diversity missing, they do not regard its lack as a problem. It makes no sense to spend extra university efforts on increasing diversity since diversity already proliferates across campus. So the issue of racial inequality raises white students' ire. Says one among many students about hypothetical scholarships for people of color:

> I don't think that that's fair. I think that's almost reverse what we're trying to do. You know, we're trying to create equality and equal diversity, but you're getting the minority more than me.

Herein we see a phenomenon in which the classic colorblind racism of believing everyone has equality of opportunity gives way to more overtly racist understandings in which whites believe themselves victimized. Since race is subsumed as just one kind of diversity, just another inconsequential difference, the centering of race in calls for social justice translates to white students as fundamentally unfair. To these white students, people of color focus on one difference among many, and unjustly demand resources because of it. Said another student, "I think affirmative action is horrible." Affirmative action to them is an unfair rigging of an otherwise equal contest. And since people of color engage in racial politics in order to game the system, whites have full license to do so too. All told, falsely advertising diversity ends up supporting racism.

Some incorrectly say the need to raise funds and the desire to support real diversity puts universities in a bind. Since universities have to raise so much more money now, partly through advertising, what can they do regarding diversity? If they don't make aspirational statements they come across as racist. If they only show white students in their glossy brochures, it looks like they embrace whiteness. If they show BIPOC students, they are deceptive.

First, we must recognize that skyrocketing tuition is the fundamental problem making all matters worse and cannot be set aside in any discussion. Raising tuition is racist: it disproportionately disadvantages people of color, both immediately and in the long term. Secondly, though contrived advertising is the most effective form of advertising, it does not have to be devoid of content. Right now, advertising aspirational diversity statements provides cover for universities. It is just an ad, right alongside other empty but catchy slogans. Instead, the university could make actual, substantive changes and advertise these. The university could critically evaluate its diverse landscape and therein implement meaningful policies and programs to confront these issues. Advertising could help turn aspirational statements into reality.

There are many good ideas and initiatives out there, such as incorporating anti-racism into the curriculum, mission, and strategic goals; establishing anti-racism centers; and setting up real mentoring programs. But the university is also in charge of its budget—already full of drastic inequalities—which could be used to help remedy racial inequality if this truly were a priority. For instance, engineering courses can cost 14 times as much as social science classes. Or to put it another way, one student's entire bachelor's degree in psychology can cost the university the same as one student taking just three classes in engineering. (And engineering is heavily male-dominated while females predominate in the social sciences). Since the university is clearly okay in using its resources to fund its engineering priorities, a much less dramatic reprioritizing of the budget to fight racism is not inconceivable. Departments could be reimbursed at a higher level for teaching BIPOC and first-generation students. They could be rewarded for making their curricula and programs better serve the most put upon students, and redress the inequalities and bigotries that increasingly plague campuses.

Currently, bold right-wing attacks openly employ race to drive their larger anti-education, increasingly totalitarian project. Instead of wasting money on branding, universities could use advertising to take a stand against these corrosive forces. Schools could show what a tremendous public good higher education is. And advertising anti-racism efforts could help universities force their opponents to out themselves as anti-anti-racist—as racist.

Periodical and Internet Sources Bibliography

The following articles have been selected to supplement the diverse views presented in this chapter.

Jonathan Guyer, "The State Department Is Still Pale, Male, and Yale," the *New Republic,* February 12, 2024. https://newrepublic.com/article/178412/state-department-diversity-blinken-stalled.

Brian Leiter, "Diversity Statements Are Still in Legal Peril," the *Chronicle of Higher Education,* June 1, 2022. www.chronicle.com/article/diversity-statements-are-still-in-legal-peril.

Adrienne Lu, "Diversity Statements Are Being Banned. Here's What Might Replace Them," the *Chronicle of Higher Education,* October 6, 2023. www.chronicle.com/article/diversity-statements-are-being-banned-heres-what-might-replace-them.

Robert Maranto and James D. Paul, "Other Than Merit: The Prevalence of Diversity, Equity, and Inclusion Statements in University Hiring," American Enterprise Institute, November 8, 2021. aei.org/research-products/report/other-than-merit-the-prevalence-of-diversity-equity-and-inclusion-statements-in-university-hiring.

Justin P. McBrayer, "Diversity Statements Are the New Faith Statements," Inside Higher Ed, May 22, 2022. https://www.insidehighered.com/views/2022/05/23/diversity-statements-are-new-faith-statements-opinion.

John McWhorter, "How Our Discussion of Race Becomes Distorted," the *New York Times,* October 1, 2021. https://www.nytimes.com/2021/10/01/opinion/language-race-semantics.html.

Pamela Paul, "Civil Discourse on Campus Is Put to the Test," the *New York Times,* March 7, 2024. https://www.nytimes.com/2024/03/07/opinion/school-dei-college-diversity.html.

Michael Powell, "D.E.I. Statements Stir Debate on College Campuses," the *New York Times,* September 8, 2023. https://www.nytimes.com/2023/09/08/us/ucla-dei-statement.html.

Christopher F. Rufo, "How We Squeezed Harvard to Push Claudine Gay Out," *Wall Street Journal,* January 3, 2024. https://www.wsj.com/articles/how-we-squeezed-harvard-claudine-gay-firing-dei-antisemitism-culture-war-a6843c4c.

Robby Soave, "Berkeley Weeded Out Job Applicants Who Didn't Propose Specific Plans to Advance Diversity," *Reason*, February 3, 2020. https://reason.com/2020/02/03/university-of-california-diversity-initiative-berkeley.

Brian Soucek, "Diversity Statements," *UC Davis Law Review*, April 2022. https://lawreview.law.ucdavis.edu/archives/55/4/diversity-statements.

Ching-Yune C. Sylvester, Laura Sánchez-Parkinson, Matthew Yettaw, and Tabbye Chavous, "The Promise of Diversity Statements: Insights and an Initial Framework Developed from a Faculty Search Process," *NCID Currents*, 2019. https://quod.lib.umich.edu/c/currents/17387731.0001.112?view=text;rgn=main.

CHAPTER 4

Is True Diversity, Equity, and Inclusion Possible?

Chapter Preface

This final set of viewpoints takes a broader look at diversity and, more specifically, equity, examining the ways that its impacts and deficits have been registered in the workplace, higher education, and society as a whole. There are many opposing opinions on whether society has become more equitable in recent years.

There are criticisms, for sure. An interesting perspective that one viewpoint in this chapter takes is looking at the ways that DEI programs have the potential to be applied internationally through multinational corporations. These companies face the challenge of applying DEI practices, which are largely impacted by values commonly held in the U.S., to other cultural contexts. Issues like these, perhaps, point to a larger issue with conceptualizing DEI in a world that is increasingly globalized, both economically and judicially.

Proponents of DEI point to the fundamental malleability of the DEI concept, the promise of diversity as an intersectional ideal. Intersectionality is the idea that a social categorizations like race, class, and gender create overlapping and, ultimately, interdependent systems of discrimination or disadvantage, but through DEI policy these intersectional differences can help ferment diversity and equity.

A world that is growing more interconnected is, implicitly, more diverse and will be pressured to become increasingly diverse in the coming years. Whether equity will be successfully incorporated into that transition is a pressing question.

VIEWPOINT 1

> "While most have made little progress, are stalled or even slipping backward, some are making impressive gains in diversity, particularly in executive teams."

There Have Been Mixed Results in the Quest for More Diverse and Inclusive Workplaces

Sundiatu Dixon-Fyle, Kevin Dolan, Dame Vivian Hunt, and Sara Prince

In this viewpoint, McKinsey consultants take stock of how successful representation efforts have been in corporate settings. The results, they say, are mixed. While more than a third of the companies in their data set still have no women on their executive teams, the report claims that the companies that do hire women appear to be doing well. Companies with more than 30 percent women executives were more likely to outperform companies where this percentage ranged from 10 to 30, according to their research. The likelihood of outperformance continues to be higher for diversity in ethnicity than for gender, the consultants add. Nevertheless, this report points to a "growing polarization between high and low performers" in terms of what companies make a point to hire women and BIPOC employees and which ones do not. McKinsey is a consulting firm that regularly puts out reports on corporate trends. Sundiatu Dixon-Fyle is a senior expert on inclusive growth and DEI in McKinsey's London office. At

"Diversity wins: How inclusion matters" by Sundiatu Dixon-Fyle, Kevin Dolan, Dame Vivian Hunt, and Sara Prince. McKinsey & Company, May 19, 2020. Reprinted with permission.

Is True Diversity, Equity, and Inclusion Possible?

the time this viewpoint was published, Kevin Dolan was a senior partner in McKinsey's Chicago office. Dame Vivian Hunt is Chief Innovation Officer at UnitedHealth Group (UHG). Sara Prince is a senior partner in McKinsey's Atlanta office.

As you read, consider the following questions:

1. What is the business case for diversity, according to this viewpoint?
2. What does this viewpoint say is the relationship between representation and outperformance?
3. Why do the authors of this viewpoint say that progress in increasing diversity has been slow?

Diversity wins is the third report in a McKinsey series investigating the business case for diversity, following *Why diversity matters* (2015) and *Delivering through diversity* (2018). Our latest report shows not only that the business case remains robust but also that the relationship between diversity on executive teams and the likelihood of financial outperformance has strengthened over time. These findings emerge from our largest data set so far, encompassing 15 countries and more than 1,000 large companies. By incorporating a "social listening" analysis of employee sentiment in online reviews, the report also provides new insights into how inclusion matters. It shows that companies should pay much greater attention to inclusion, even when they are relatively diverse.

By following the trajectories of hundreds of companies in our data set since 2014, we find that the overall slow growth in diversity often observed in fact masks a growing polarization among these organizations. While most have made little progress, are stalled or even slipping backward, some are making impressive gains in diversity, particularly in executive teams. We show that these diversity winners are adopting systematic,

Diversity, Equity, and Inclusion

business-led approaches to inclusion and diversity (I&D). And, with a special focus on inclusion, we highlight the areas where companies should take far bolder action to create a long-lasting inclusive culture and to promote inclusive behavior.

A Stronger Business Case for Diversity, but Slow Progress Overall

Our latest analysis reaffirms the strong business case for both gender diversity and ethnic and cultural diversity in corporate leadership—and shows that this business case continues to strengthen. The most diverse companies are now more likely than ever to outperform less diverse peers on profitability.

Our 2019 analysis finds that companies in the top quartile for gender diversity on executive teams were 25 percent more likely to have above-average profitability than companies in the fourth quartile—up from 21 percent in 2017 and 15 percent in 2014.

Moreover, we found that the greater the representation, the higher the likelihood of outperformance. Companies with more than 30 percent women executives were more likely to outperform companies where this percentage ranged from 10 to 30, and in turn these companies were more likely to outperform those with even fewer women executives, or none at all. A substantial differential likelihood of outperformance—48 percent—separates the most from the least gender-diverse companies.

In the case of ethnic and cultural diversity, our business-case findings are equally compelling: in 2019, top-quartile companies outperformed those in the fourth one by 36 percent in profitability, slightly up from 33 percent in 2017 and 35 percent in 2014. As we have previously found, the likelihood of outperformance continues to be higher for diversity in ethnicity than for gender.

Yet progress, overall, has been slow. In the companies in our original 2014 data set, based in the United States and the United

Kingdom, female representation on executive teams rose from 15 percent in 2014 to 20 percent in 2019. Across our global data set, for which our data starts in 2017, gender diversity moved up just one percentage point—to 15 percent, from 14—in 2019. More than a third of the companies in our data set still have no women at all on their executive teams. This lack of material progress is evident across all industries and in most countries. Similarly, the representation of ethnic-minorities on UK and US executive teams stood at only 13 percent in 2019, up from just 7 percent in 2014. For our global data set, this proportion was 14 percent in 2019, up from 12 percent in 2017.

The Widening Gap Between Winners and Laggards

While overall progress on gender and cultural representation has been slow, this is not consistent across all organizations. Our research clearly shows that there is a widening gap between I&D leaders and companies that have yet to embrace diversity. A third of the companies we analyzed have achieved real gains in top-team diversity over the five-year period. But most have made little or no progress, and some have even gone backward.

This growing polarization between high and low performers is reflected in an increased likelihood of a performance penalty. In 2019, fourth-quartile companies for gender diversity on executive teams were 19 percent more likely than companies in the other three quartiles to underperform on profitability—up from 15 percent in 2017 and 9 percent in 2015. At companies in the fourth quartile for both gender and ethnic diversity, the penalty was even steeper in 2019: they were 27 percent more likely to underperform on profitability than all other companies in our data set.

We sought to understand how companies in our original 2014 data set have been progressing, and in doing so we identified five cohorts. These were based on their starting points and speed of progress on executive team gender representation and, separately, ethnic-minority representation. In the first two cohorts, Diversity Leaders and Fast Movers, diverse representation improved strongly over the past five years: for example, gender Fast Movers have almost quadrupled the representation of women on executive teams, to 27 percent, in 2019; for ethnicity, companies in the equivalent cohort have increased their level of diversity from just 1 percent in 2014 to 18 percent in 2019.

At the other end of the spectrum, the already poor diversity performance of the Laggards has declined further. In 2019, an average of 8 percent of executive team members at these companies were female—and they had no ethnic-minority representation at all. The two other cohorts are Moderate Movers, which have on average experienced a slower improvement in diversity, and Resting on Laurels, which started with higher levels of diversity than Laggards did, but have similarly become less diverse since 2014.

We also found that the average likelihood of financial outperformance in these cohorts is consistent with our findings in the quartile analysis above. For example, in 2019, companies in the Resting on Laurels cohort on average had the highest likelihood of outperformance on profitability, at almost 62 percent—likely reflecting their historically high levels of diversity on executive teams. Laggards, on the other hand, are more likely to underperform their national industry median in profitability, at 40 percent.

How Inclusion Matters

By analyzing surveys and company research, we explored how different approaches to I&D could have shaped the trajectories of the companies in our data set. Our work suggested two critical factors: a systematic business-led approach to I&D, and bold action on inclusion. On the former we have previously advocated for an I&D approach based on a robust business case tailored to the

Is True Diversity, Equity, and Inclusion Possible?

needs of individual companies, evidenced-based targets, and core-business leadership accountability.

To further understand how inclusion matters—and which aspects of it employees regard as significant—we conducted our first analysis of inclusion-related indicators. We conducted this outside-in using "social listening," focusing on sentiment in employee reviews of their employers posted on US-based online platforms.

While this approach is indicative, rather than conclusive, it could provide a more candid read on inclusion than internal employee-satisfaction surveys do—and makes it possible to analyze data across dozens of companies rapidly and simultaneously. We focused on three industries with the highest levels of executive-team diversity in our data set: financial services, technology, and healthcare. In these sectors, comments directly pertaining to I&D accounted for around one-third of total comments made, suggesting that this topic is high on employees' minds.

We analyzed comments relating to five indicators. The first two—diverse representation and leadership accountability for I&D—are evidence of a systematic approach to I&D. The other three—equality, openness, and belonging—are core components of inclusion. For several of these indicators, our findings suggest "pain points" in the experience of employees:

- While overall sentiment on diversity was 52 percent positive and 31 percent negative, sentiment on inclusion was markedly worse, at only 29 percent positive and 61 percent negative. This encapsulates the challenge that even the more diverse companies still face in tackling inclusion. Hiring diverse talent isn't enough—it's the workplace experience that shapes whether people remain and thrive.

- Opinions about leadership and accountability in I&D accounted for the highest number of mentions and were

strongly negative. On average, across industries, 51 percent of the total mentions related to leadership, and 56 percent of those were negative. This finding underscores the increasingly recognized need for companies to improve their I&D engagement with core-business managers.
- For the three indicators of inclusion—equality, openness, and belonging—we found particularly high levels of negative sentiment about equality and fairness of opportunity. Negative sentiment about equality ranged from 63 to 80 percent across the industries analyzed. The work environment's openness, which encompasses bias and discrimination, was also a significant concern—negative sentiment across industries ranged from 38 to 56 percent. Belonging elicited overall positive sentiment, but from a relatively small number of mentions.

These findings highlight the importance not just of inclusion overall but also of specific aspects of inclusion. Even relatively diverse companies face significant challenges in creating work environments characterized by inclusive leadership and accountability among managers, equality and fairness of opportunity, and openness and freedom from bias and discrimination.

Winning Through Inclusion and Diversity: Taking Bold Action

We took a close look at our data set's more diverse companies, which as we have seen are more likely to outperform financially. The common thread for these diversity leaders is a systematic approach and bold steps to strengthen inclusion. Drawing on best practices from these companies, this report highlights five areas of action:
- Ensure the representation of diverse talent. This is still an essential driver of inclusion. Companies should focus on advancing diverse talent into executive, management, technical, and board roles. They should ensure that a robust

Is True Diversity, Equity, and Inclusion Possible?

I&D business case designed for individual companies is well accepted and think seriously about which forms of multivariate diversity to prioritize (for example, going beyond gender and ethnicity). They also need to set the right data-driven targets for the representation of diverse talent.
- Strengthen leadership accountability and capabilities for I&D. Companies should place their core-business leaders and managers at the heart of the I&D effort—beyond the HR function or employee resource-group leaders. In addition, they should not only strengthen the inclusive-leadership capabilities of their managers and executives but also more emphatically hold all leaders to account for progress on I&D.
- Enable equality of opportunity through fairness and transparency. To advance toward a true meritocracy, it is critical that companies ensure a level playing field in advancement and opportunity. They should deploy analytics tools to show that promotions, pay processes, and the criteria behind them, are transparent and fair; debias these processes; and strive to meet diversity targets in their long-term workforce plans.
- Promote openness and tackle microaggressions. Companies should uphold a zero-tolerance policy for discriminatory behavior, such as bullying and harassment, and actively help managers and staff to identify and address microaggressions. They should also establish norms for open, welcoming behavior and ask leaders and employees to assess each other on how they are living up to that standard.
- Foster belonging through unequivocal support for multivariate diversity. Companies should build a culture where all employees feel they can bring their whole selves to work. Managers should communicate and visibly embrace their commitment to multivariate forms of

diversity, building a connection to a wide range of people and supporting employee resource groups to foster a sense of community and belonging. Companies should explicitly assess belonging in internal surveys.

VIEWPOINT

> *"The diversity, equity, and inclusion (DEI) bureaucracy is the nemesis of the Enlightenment ideal of knowledge."*

Merit Should Be Prioritized Over Diversity

Heather Mac Donald

In this critical take on DEI initiatives, Heather Mac Donald argues that diversity policies at institutions of higher learning have a negative impact and create less successful students in their efforts to increase diversity. The problem, she writes, is not with college courses, but racial differences in academic performance. These differences begin in high school and the "gaps do not subsequently close in college but are replicated in every graduate measure of academic skills," she argues, suggesting that creating opportunities for more diverse students does not lead to greater academic success for them. She argues that universities should focus on a colorblind definition of academic excellence and merit instead. Heather Mac Donald is a fellow of the Manhattan Institute, a conservative think tank, and author of the book When Race Trumps Merit.

As you read, consider the following questions:

1. What does Mac Donald consider the Enlightenment ideal of universal knowledge?

"Merit Over Identity: Dismantling DEI bureaucracies is the key to reviving American universities" by Heather Mac Donald. Manhattan Institute for Policy Research, Inc., April 11, 2023. Reprinted with permission.

2. In what ways do DEI programs conflict with this Enlightenment ideal, according to this viewpoint?
3. What problems does the author have with the first step of the United States Medical Licensing Exam?

I start from the following proposition: being female is not an accomplishment. My being female should play no role in my being hired for a job. Of course, my sex undoubtedly has made me the target of sex preferences on numerous occasions, thus casting doubt on any actual qualifications I might presume to possess.

My being female should be particularly irrelevant in a university. Until recently, universities were dedicated to the Enlightenment ideal of universal knowledge. A male Chinese engineer and a female Nigerian engineer may have no spoken language in common, but they can communicate through the universal languages of mathematics and physics. Whether the buildings they erect stand or fall depends not on their nationality or sex but on their mastery of engineering principles.

I will go further. Being Black, gay, or gender-fluid are also not accomplishments, and should have nothing to do with faculty hiring or student admissions. The only thing that should matter when, say, a medical school hires a researcher in pancreatic cancer is whether that oncologist is the best in his field.

The diversity, equity, and inclusion (DEI) bureaucracy is the nemesis of the Enlightenment ideal of knowledge. It puts relentless pressure on every academic department to hire on the basis of race and sex, not on the basis of intellectual achievement. Every faculty search today is a desperate effort to find even remotely qualified minority or female candidates. Being female or a non-Asian minority confers an enormous advantage in the hiring and tenure process.

Yet despite this obsessive attention to diversity, many departments still do not pass the DEI proportionality test. So DEI bureaucrats are on a crusade to extirpate the sources of bias that allegedly stand in the way of proportional representation. Every colorblind objective test of academic skills—SAT, LSAT, or MCAT—is under attack as racist and is going down.

Consider Step One of the United States Medical Licensing Exam, which tests students' knowledge of basic physiological processes. Step One changed to a pass-fail grading system last year because Black and Hispanic students disproportionately got low scores, impeding their ability to land the residency of their choice. Whether the students who will now squeak by with a pass are the most qualified candidates for those residencies is of no interest to the gatekeepers.

Scientific institutions are now reformulating research priorities to increase the diversity of federal grant recipients. The National Institutes of Health has shifted funding from basic science to research on health disparities and racism simply because Black scientists do more research on these race topics and less on pure science.

Reality check: the reason why colleges are not proportionally diverse has nothing to do with bias or exclusion. The reason is large racial differences in academic skills. This is an uncomfortable subject, and one that is taboo on college campuses, but if we are going to indict American universities and other institutions for systemic racism, we should get our facts straight.

In 2019, according to the National Assessment of Educational Progress, 66 percent of Black 12th-graders did not possess even partial mastery of basic 12th-grade math skills, such as being able to perform arithmetical calculations or to recognize a linear function on a graph. Only 7 percent of Black 12th-graders were competent on those basic 12th-grade math skills, and the number who were advanced was too small to show up statistically. The picture was not much better in reading.

In 2021, the American College Testing organization rated only 10 percent of Black high school seniors as college ready, based on their combined math, general science, and reading scores on the ACT. Whites were five times as likely to be college ready.

Diversity, Equity, and Inclusion

These gaps do not subsequently close in college but are replicated in every graduate measure of academic skills. They mean that, at present, you can have diversity, or you can have meritocracy. You cannot have both. It is mathematically impossible to produce 13 percent Black representation in chemistry, nuclear biology, or medicine, say, without lowering meritocratic standards.

Of course, there are many individuals from underrepresented groups who meet existing standards. Far from being discriminated against, however, they are treated like "gold dust," as an astrophysicist in the University of California told me.

Thanks to DEI ideology, we are opting for diversity over meritocracy. Indeed, diversity is simply a code word for preferences. But those preferences do not do their alleged beneficiaries any favors.

If MIT admitted me for the sake of gender diversity and I had a 600 on my math SAT while most of my nonpreferred peers had close to a perfect 800, I would struggle in, if not fail, my math classes, because the teaching would be pitched to the class average. I would likely have done perfectly well, however, at a school where my peers matched my own level of academic preparation.

So, too, for the recipients of race preferences. They would be academically competitive in colleges where their qualifications matched those of their peers, but when they are catapulted into schools for which they are not prepared, they struggle, as numerous studies have documented. Racial-preference beneficiaries intending to major in STEM are far more likely to switch out of their intended major than their nonpreferred peers. The DEI bureaucracy then informs them that their academic difficulties are the result of their school's systemic racism. The solution to their struggles is of course to increase the size and power of the diversity bureaucracy.

Indeed, we are witnessing at this very moment a great institutional mitosis, as existing DEI bureaucracies spawn identical bureaucracies. These latter go under a new name, however: "offices of belonging." If you thought that "inclusion" encompassed belonging, you underestimate DEI's fecundity in generating new sinecures.

A university's task is the pursuit of truth. The DEI bureaucracy, however, is founded on a lie—one that teaches students to think of themselves as victims and to see racism where none exists. It is iatrogenic, creating through racial preferences the very divisions and discomfort that it purports to solve, in an endless, vicious circle.

By all means, let us redouble our efforts to make sure that all children are prepared to succeed, by focusing on a child's earliest years. Campus diversity bureaucrats have nothing to contribute to that effort. They do, however, suck up vast sums of money, narrow the acceptable range of discourse, and force the adoption of double standards of achievement.

The university should embrace a single colorblind definition of excellence. It will only do so, however, by eliminating DEI fiefdoms and by replacing identity with merit as the touchstone of academic accomplishment.

VIEWPOINT 3

> "Global trans health equity means providing resources to target the root causes of gender-based health disparities. This involves legal gender recognition, government support and anti-discrimination laws."

Global Health Equity Goes Beyond the Appearance of Diversity

Reya Farber

In this viewpoint Reya Farber makes the argument that achieving equity isn't just important in professional and academic spaces—it is also essential in health care. She frames her discussion of health equity around the treatment of transgender people around the world. While trans visibility has increased in recent years, many global health organizations still do not acknowledge the needs of gender-diverse people, and there is little research on the health issues that impact trans people. The goal of global health equity in this context would be to make sure trans people in all countries have access to equitable and culturally competent care. Furthermore, trans people and other marginalized groups should have a greater say in decisions around global health. These policies would not only benefit trans people, but would create better health outcomes for other marginalized groups as

"Health Rights for Trans People Varies Widely Around the Globe—Achieving Trans Bliss and Joy Will Require Equity, Social Respect and Legal Protections," by Reya Farber, The Conversation, November 16, 2022, https://theconversation.com/health-rights-for-trans-people-vary-widely-around-the-globe-achieving-trans-bliss-and-joy-will-require-equity-social-respect-and-legal-protections-194237. Licensed under CC BY-ND 4.0 International.

Is True Diversity, Equity, and Inclusion Possible?

well. Reya Farber is an assistant professor of sociology at the College of William & Mary in Williamsburg, Virginia.

As you read, consider the following questions:

1. According to this viewpoint, what percent of global health-related organizations do not explicitly reference gender-diverse people (such as trans people) in their work?
2. What countries mentioned in this viewpoint criminalize trans people?
3. According to Farber, what does decolonizing global health mean?

While transgender people might be more culturally recognized in the U.S. than ever, visibility is not the same as justice.

Transgender is an umbrella category that emerged in the U.S. in the 1990s to encompass diverse gender identities that don't fully correspond with an individual's assigned sex at birth. Although local communities worldwide have adopted this term, it can also erase and collapse other diverse gender identities people have used across time, location and culture.

People who are today called trans, nonbinary and intersex have existed for centuries throughout the world. The rights of trans people have not always been up for debate in mainstream society, and nonnormative sex and gender categories appear in ancient Buddhist texts, as well as Jewish rabbinic literature. Yet colonial conquests have violently stamped out sexual and gender diversity globally.

Trans people's right to exist has been challenged throughout time and across the world in multiple ways. Worldwide, trans people face disparities across many areas, including access to health care, legal support and economic security. Governments, global organizations and the legacies of colonialism also enact high levels of violence and stigma against them.

At the same time, 95% of global health-related organizations do not recognize or mention the needs of gender-diverse people in their work, resulting in the "near-universal exclusion" of trans people from health practices and policies. There is also a lack of holistic trans-inclusive research around the world. For instance, searching for the word "transgender" on the website for the Institute for Health Metrics and Evaluation, the global health metrics giant of the Bill and Melinda Gates Foundation that collaborates with the World Health Organization to improve global health data, currently returns zero results.

As a sociologist, I study how health outcomes are affected by various social conditions, including global economic policies, institutions and cultural values. In particular, I analyzed how

> ## WHAT IS HEALTH EQUITY?
>
> In a report designed to increase consensus around meaning of health equity, the Robert Wood Johnson Foundation (RWJF) provides the following definition: "Health equity means that everyone has a fair and just opportunity to be as healthy as possible. This requires removing obstacles to health such as poverty, discrimination, and their consequences, including powerlessness and lack of access to good jobs with fair pay, quality education and housing, safe environments, and health care."
>
> Health equity surrounds and underpins RWJF's vision of a society in which everyone has an equal opportunity to live the healthiest life possible. The authors, including RWJF staff members, put forth these four key steps to achieve health equity: Identify important health disparities. Many disparities in health are rooted in inequities in the opportunities and resources needed to be as healthy as possible. The determinants of health include living and working conditions, education, income, neighborhood characteristic, social inclusion, and medical care. An increase in opportunities to

government-endorsed medical tourism, or health-related travel, has affected Thai transgender women. Broadly, I seek to understand how the body acts as what French philosopher Michel Foucault calls an "inscribed surface of events," imprinted upon by an ever-changing social context that can afford or withhold resources, rights, recognition and power.

With their health and well-being shaped by the social context worldwide, the bodies of transgender people are no exception.

History of Gender-Affirming Care

Medical institutions and authorities are a major pathway to health and how one lives in one's body. They define, classify and pathologize a range of human conditions, from male pattern baldness to fatness.

> be healthier will benefit everyone but more focus should be placed on groups that have been excluded or marginalized in the past.
> - Change and implement policies, laws, systems, environments, and practices to reduce inequities in the opportunities and resources needed to be as healthy as possible. Eliminate the unfair individual and institutional social conditions that give rise to the inequities.
> - Evaluate and monitor efforts using short- and long-term measures as it may take decades or generations to reduce some health disparities. In order not to underestimate the size of the gap between advantaged and disadvantaged, disadvantaged groups should not be compared to the general population but to advantaged groups.
> - Reassess strategies in light of process and outcomes and plan next steps. Actively engage those most affected by disparities in the identification, design, implementation, and evaluation of promising solutions
>
> "What is Health Equity?" by Braveman P, Arkin E, Orleans T, Proctor D, Plough A, Robert Wood Johnson Foundation, May 1, 2017.

The German physician Magnus Hirschfeld coined the now antiquated term "transvestite" in 1910 to define those who desired to express themselves in opposition to their sex assigned at birth. At his Institute for Sexual Science, Hirschfeld offered people hormone therapy and performed the first documented genital transformation surgery. Adolf Hitler deemed Hirschfeld "the most dangerous Jew in Germany," and the Nazis burned his research center after he fled for his life.

Despite this violence toward trans medicine, endocrinology in the U.S. and Europe advanced in the 1930s with the use of synthetic testosterone and estrogen for medical transitioning. Estrogen was first purified in 1923 and used for hot flashes, bone loss prevention and other reproductive health issues. Testosterone was isolated and synthesized in 1935 and first used to treat hypogonadism in men as well as tumor growth in women.

Puberty blockers, or gonadotropin-releasing hormone agonists, were first approved by the U.S. FDA in 1993 for children undergoing puberty too early. For trans adolescents experiencing gender dysphoria, or distress from a mismatch between their gender identity and sex assigned at birth, these medications can be critically important for their well-being. Far from being experimental, the medications have strong evidence for their overall beneficial effects for trans youths.

Christine Jorgensen was the first American to undergo what was then called "sex change" surgery, in Denmark in 1952, making headline news. Doctors in other parts of the world also started to gain clinical expertise in vaginoplasty, sparking global networks of transgender health care. For instance, surgeons in Thailand developed their own techniques in the 1970s for Thai trans women.

Soon, trans people from other countries learned of Thai surgical techniques and began to travel to Thailand for care. With strong government support, Thailand has become a global hub for gender-affirming services. Subsequently, foreign travelers "crowded out" some Thai trans people from quality care as the market shifted to accommodate medical tourists.

For some health travelers, services are more affordable in Thailand than in their home country. Traveling for health services can also provide greater anonymity. For those in the U.K. seeking gender-affirming care, traveling abroad is an alternative to long wait times.

Medical tourism is more dire for those living in countries where trans people face criminalization, such as Brunei, Lebanon and Malawi, or where gender-affirming surgeries are religiously prohibited, such as Saudi Arabia.

What Does Global Health Equity Mean?

Globally, trans people experience issues accessing culturally competent and equitable health care services, both generally and for gender-affirming services. Trans and gender-diverse people experience greater mental distress and everyday violence and discrimination than their cisgender peers.

A 2019 report of nearly 200 health organizations around the world found that 93% do not recognize trans people in their work on gender equality, and 92% do not mention trans health in their programmatic services. Decolonizing global health means including marginalized people in decisions and knowledge production around global health. It also includes and addresses the needs of trans and gender-diverse people worldwide.

Global trans health equity means providing resources to target the root causes of gender-based health disparities. This involves legal gender recognition, government support and anti-discrimination laws. While medical and public health support is necessary for trans women, who are disproportionately affected by HIV worldwide, global trans health equity also means addressing other areas that contribute to this disparity, such as poverty, economic exclusion and workplace discrimination.

For countries with universal health coverage, medical and public health researchers recommend that gender-affirming services be included as essential services. They are not cosmetic, but are necessary for those who want them.

Better Alternatives for All

Amid everyday injustices, violence and vulnerabilities are countless forms of trans resilience and resistance, activism, collective care and knowledge sharing. There are even some "bubble[s] of utopia," or clinics and health care settings where trans people can access services with reduced delay. These alternatives open the possibility for transgender bliss, or liberation from restrictive colonial gender constructs, and transgender joy, or improving one's quality of life and forming meaningful connections by embracing a marginalized identity.

How can policies, institutions and society cultivate trans bliss and joy worldwide?

All human bodies are "sociocultural artifacts." How they are expressed and lived in is determined by social contexts and shaped by available resources. Sex and gender are points in a vast "multi-dimensional space" of anatomy, hormones, chromosomes, environment and culture. Global health equity for trans people holds accountable the institutions and decision-makers responsible for the health and safety of all human beings. It is oriented toward the freedom to flourish in a world that celebrates sex and gender diversity as a natural fact of life.

VIEWPOINT 4

> *"If the difference between diversity and inclusion is analogous to being invited to the party (i.e., diversity) versus being asked to dance (i.e., inclusion), then belonging can be achieved by having the opportunity to dance to the beat of one's own drum or at least to one's own soundtrack."*

There Are Many Advantages to Incorporating DEI in International Organizations

William Newburry, Matevž (Matt) Rašković, Saba S. Colakoglu, Maria Alejandra Gonzalez-Perez, and Dana Minbaeva

In this viewpoint, which is the introduction to a journal issue on DEI in the workplace, the authors look at some of larger challenges to implementing DEI at the organizational level, especially internationally. They argue that there are few organizations that have managed to holistically implement DEI, pointing to some of the "double-edged" problems that have resulted from the way in which those polices have been implemented. On the other hand, the report notes that DEI efforts have in recent years become more intersectional, which has helped them adapt to different social situations. William

Newburry, W., Rašković, M. (Matt), Colakoglu, S. S., Gonzalez-Perez, M. A., & Minbaeva, D. 2022. Diversity, Equity and Inclusion in International Business: Dimensions and Challenges. AIB Insights, 22(3). https://doi.org/10.46697/001c.36582. Licensed under CC BY 4.0.

Newberry is a Ryder Eminent Scholar of Global Business and a professor of international business at Florida International University. Matevž (Matt) Rašković is an associate professor of international business at Auckland University of Technology in New Zealand. Saba S. Colakoglu is a senior lecturer in the organizational behavior group at the Scheller College of Business at Georgia Institute of Technology. Maria Alejandra Gonzalez-Perez is a distinguished professor of corporate sustainability at Universidad EAFIT in Colombia. Dana Minbaeva is a professor of strategic human capital at King's Business School of King's College of London, UK.

As you read, consider the following questions:

1. What are some of the positive organizational outcomes that this viewpoint highlights?
2. How does this viewpoint contend that diversity can also act as a double-edged sword?
3. In what way does this viewpoint argue that organizations can take cues from their institutional environments?

Calls to address diversity, equity and inclusion (DEI) have become common in almost all corners around the globe—whether they relate to gender identity, race, ethnicity, sexual orientation, indigenous identity and ancestry background, religion, (dis)ability, neurological profile, language, immigration status and/or a host of other socially constructed categories. However, while DEI initiatives have been around in the corporate world for decades, they have been primarily limited to human resource management and guided by either a discrimination-and-fairness logic or an access-and-legitimacy logic (Thomas & Ely, 1996). Few organizations have been able to holistically embed DEI at an advanced level, harnessing its learning and strategic potential (Ely & Thomas, 2020; Georgiadou, Gonzalez-Perez, &

Olivas-Luján, 2019a, 2019b). In an increasingly polarized world fraught with turbulence, one in which we face the same storms but can find ourselves in very different boats, addressing DEI at an organizational and industry level is becoming an important part of a bigger puzzle of creating what Martin Sandbu (2020) calls an "economy of belonging" that works for everyone, not just some. According to Verna Myers, a well-known inclusion strategist and thought leader, DEI is a little bit like dancing. However, if the difference between diversity and inclusion is analogous to being invited to the party (i.e., diversity) versus being asked to dance (i.e., inclusion), then belonging can be achieved by having the opportunity to dance to the beat of one's own drum or at least to one's own soundtrack. As organizations and business leaders pursue a deeper purpose, one in which high performance is driven by "heart and soul" (Gulati, 2022), DEI strategies can help pave the way to (re)building an economy of belonging at a global level to makes sure globalization doesn't go "bump in the night" (Kobrin, 2020). Given this important need, we are happy to present this special issue of AIB Insights on "Diversity, Equity and Inclusion in International Business" to provide some guidance across these efforts.

Examining DEI in an international business setting highlights the fact that influences on DEI occur across multiple, often embedded levels. We can consider DEI policy influences occurring at a global influence level (e.g., from the U.N.) down to within-firm team dynamics and even within individuals, as well as many levels in-between. These multi-level DEI influences create different forms of pressure on firms operating in a multinational context and tensions that people, organizations and communities need to reconcile. For example, at the country-level, DEI scholars have made inroads into understanding how societies differ in their abilities to recognize, tolerate, and adapt to various types of (social) differences and diversity (e.g., Zanakis, Newburry, & Taras, 2016). These differences could influence the degree to which various DEI polices of multinationals are accepted within a particular society. Similarly, a recent study of LGBT inclusion across 132 countries has shown a clear link between LGBT inclusion and economic development (Badgett, Waaldijk, & van der Meulen Rodgers, 2019). While the direction of causality warrants more examining, it does suggest that national-level DEI policies are associated with economic advancement, which could have firm-level implications.

At the organizational level, DEI has been linked to a series of positive organizational outcomes which include higher creativity, greater adaptability and better problem-solving (Stahl, Tung, Kostova, & Zellmer-Bruhn, 2016). Yet, research coming from social psychology shows that diversity can also act as a double-edged sword through mechanisms of social categorization, attraction based on similarity, information processing and decision making (e.g., Carter & Phillips, 2017). For example, when DEI initiatives lead to minimization of biases and reduced social categorization, members within more diverse groups might focus more on tasks and engage in more effortful information processing in order to address opinions about those tasks arising from greater diversity within the group (Carter & Phillips, 2017).

In line with the so-called learning-and-effectiveness paradigm (Ely & Thomas, 2020), DEI might become an important strategic puzzle piece in how societies, organizations and communities navigate a world with increasing volatility, uncertainty, complexity, and ambiguity (VUCA) and a post-Pandemic "New Normal." Yet, at the same time, it is important not to see DEI as a silver-bullet end, but a means to many different ends.

It is also important to note that organizations take cues from their institutional environments, while also having the potential to impact them in a process of social structuration where structure and agency interact. Multinationals may be important players in this influence as they carry corporate policies to new countries, becoming cross-pollinators, as well as agents of (institutional) change.

Exploring the multi-level influences on DEI within multinational organizations provides opportunities for IB scholars to integrate country-level research on various types of distance (e.g., cultural, psychic, semantic etc.) with primarily firm-level and within-firm research on diversity. Yet, only recently, have we begun to approach distance in conjunction with diversity (e.g., Stahl et al., 2016). Both distance and diversity are conceptually close, acting as "two sides of the same coin" (Doh, 2021). The former captures differences between countries, the latter differences between individuals (Lumineau, Hanisch, & Wurtz, 2021). The diversity literature offers nuance and sophistication which can revitalize traditional approaches to distance within international business (IB), infusing it with much needed actionable insights (Doh, 2021).

Of particular interest to the IB community is how internationalization and diversity issues interact in multinational companies (e.g., Hermans et al., 2017). Issues like the social construction of gender differences (e.g., Koveshnikov, Tienari, & Piekkari, 2019), the use of language and gender marking (e.g., Shoham, 2019), or managing and stigmatization of LGBT expatriates (e.g., Moeller & Maley, 2018), are just some of the areas of research in recent years. Multinational organizations are also social spaces and transnational communities (Morgan & Kristensen, 2006). They act as sites for identity politics, are part of identity building processes, take on broad social issues and can take on the role of change agents (Vaara, Tienari, & Koveshnikov, 2021). This calls for a better understanding of sources, outcomes, and intersectionality of social identities and diversity types in multinational organizations (Rašković, 2021). Intersectionality, which refers to the intersection and interaction of various types of social identities becomes a particularly difficult and important issue in international contexts given that different diversity elements may be perceived or may manifest themselves differently in different geographic contexts. Similarly, as in the case of distance, the "magic" happens not along independent dimensions of distance or diversity, but at their intersection and interaction. While it is beyond the scope of this issue introduction to delve more deeply into all of these topics, we believe they open up a wide range of important areas and questions to explore. It shows us that DEI research doesn't just have a place within the IB discipline, but that DEI research can also help advance several areas of theorizing and research within the IB discipline in turn.

Articles and Practitioner Interview

Looking at the articles in this special issue, we have seven articles and one additional practitioner interview. The first four articles look at DEI issues in a broader sense. Two of these articles examine DEI issues related to refugees and migration issues, followed by two that examine institutional characteristics influencing DEI practices. The last three articles and our practitioner interview focus on individual diversity dimensions. Two of these relate to gender. A focus on gender is consistent with gender equality being goal number 5 of the 17 United Nations Sustainable Development Goals (SDGs). The next article in the issue examines neurodiversity as it relates to being differently abled in MNCs. Finally, we conclude with an interview with Ramkrishna (Ram) Sinha, co-Founder of the Pride Circle. Pride Circle is India's largest social enterprise in the LGBT+ space. Ram shares his experience and advice addressing DEI issues related to MNC operations in emerging markets, both specifically in relation to the LGBT+ community, as well as more generally. We briefly overview each of these articles below. We hope you enjoy these articles, and that they inspire the readers in their DEI activities.

Within this issue, we also note a lack of race-based diversity articles. We wonder if this relates to the difficulties of examining race in a global context, where understandings of what constitute racial differences vary widely. We also see great opportunity for future study of the intersectionality of DEI dimensions in international contexts. Lastly, we also hope that as the broader management discipline advances in its decolonization efforts, future research on DEI issues within the AIB community will also include the overlooked indigenous voices and their stories (Banerjee, 2022; Bruton, Zahra, Van de Ven, & Hitt, 2022).

Refugees and Migration

The first two articles in this issue examine DEI issues related to refugees and migration, two highly important topics in the current global environment. The article "How Multinational Corporations Can Support Refugee Workforce Integration: Empathize Globally, Strategize Locally" is by Betina Szkudlarek and Priya Roy from the University of Sydney, Australia, and Eun Su Lee from the University of Newcastle, Australia. The authors examine the role of refugees in recruitment strategies, and how hiring refugees can not only result in quality employees, but also contributes to DEI strategies. Using the case of IKEA, they demonstrate how the interaction of localization and global strategies can be used by MNCs to develop sustainable refugee workforce integration solutions.

Tanvi Kothari of San Jose State University, USA, Maria Elo of the University of Southern Denmark, and Nila Wiese of the University of Puget Sound, USA, authored the article "Born as a Citizen and Reborn as an Alien: Migrant Diversity in Global Business." The authors note how mass migration has contributed to changes in racial, ethnic and other compositions of modern societies, which has resulted in the creation of superdiversity. They then incorporate various diversity lenses in order to focus attention on managerial and policy areas that need attention to enhance firms' competitiveness and the social cohesion of migrants. In doing so, they bring to the forefront the topic of migrant superdiversity as an important consideration in our understanding of equity and inclusion.

Institutional Influences

The next two articles examine institutional influences on DEI practices. Visalakshy Sasikala and Venkataraman Sankaranarayanan of the Indian Institute of Management Kozhikode authored "Diversity in Global Mining: Where We Are and What We Need to Do." In this article, the authors examine the diversity statements and initiatives of 25 of the top 50 global mining firms in order to better understand diversity in this historically male-dominated industry. The authors find that home country organizational field configurations influence how mining firms perceive diversity along with the specific diversity dimensions they focus their attention on. More specifically, the authors distinguish between accommodative, defensive and reactive configurations to understand regional variations in how mining firms manage diversity.

"Institutional Distance versus Intra-Country Differences: Capturing and Leveraging the Diversity Within" is written by Susan Perkins from New York University, USA. The field of international business (IB) largely focuses on inter-country institutional differences. However, very little focus and attention have been given to the social interactions of sub-cultural groups within a country. Dr. Perkins asks whether we could be overlooking opportunities to better understand diversity within countries and how these differences can be leveraged to benefit firm performance? This article also aims to provide insights on how IB scholars, managers, and educators can engage further in developing strategies that achieve more diverse and equitable societal and economic outcomes.

Individual Diversity Dimensions

The next two articles in this issue examine topics related to Gender and DEI. The first, "It Is All in Their Positioning: Academic Women's Silence in Iran", is by Leila Lotfi Dehkharghani of Ferdowsi University of Mashhad, Iran, Jane Menzies and Harsh Suri of Deakin University, Australia, and Yaghoob Maharati of Ferdowsi University of Mashhad, Iran. Noting that Iran ranks 150 out of 156 in the World Economic Forum's Global Gender Gap Survey, the authors use positioning theory to identify and explain storylines regarding appropriate roles for women in Iran which contribute to their silence in academic settings. They argue that women's silence in Iran is reinforced by their macro, meso and organizational environments, which collectively constrain their self-esteem and self-confidence. The authors then provide recommendations to local and international organizations operating in Iran to help in the process of creating new storylines to counteract the pressures on women towards silence.

Suparna Chakraborty of the University of San Francisco, USA, and Ryka Chopra from Mission San Jose High School, USA, authored "Transcending Cheap Talk in Female Entrepreneurship: Cross-Country Evidence." The authors note that while it is common for nations to have policies empowering women, it is questionable whether these policies are effective in encouraging female entrepreneurship and that a gap remains between policy enactment and enforcement. The authors then examine cross-country differences in female entrepreneurship and relate them to political, workplace and social domains, providing policy suggestions within each of these three domains.

Dana L. Ott of Otago Business School, University of Otago, New Zealand, and Emily Russo and Miriam Moeller of UQ Business School, University of Queensland, Australia, wrote "Neurodiversity, Equity, and Inclusion in MNCs." The authors address the issue of neurodiversity, which they describe by noting that "the idea that neurological differences that have traditionally been considered atypical are normal variations of the human genome – essentially, neurodivergent individuals are simply differently abled." They then further specify how neurodiversity is an invisible form of inequality in most MNCs, and how neurodiversity inclusion challenges these companies. The authors conclude by providing guidance to MNCs and their international human resource management leaders regarding integrating neurodiversity initiatives into their DEI agendas, which they suggest will ultimately help improve MNC effectiveness and performance.

Practitioner Interview

We conclude this issue with a practitioner interview. In "Building Bridges Between (Global) Business and the Rainbow Community in India: An Interview with Pride Circle's Co-Founder Ramkrishna Sinha," Matevž (Matt) Rašković of Auckland University of Technology in New Zealand interviews Ramkrishna (Ram) Sinha, the Co-Founder of Pride Circle in India. Established in 2017, Pride Circle is India's largest LGBT+ focused social enterprise and one of the largest players in the DEI space within Asia. Ram challenges Ely and Thomas' (2020) recent call to move beyond making a business case for DEI to organizations. As long as business is done, there also has to be a business case for DEI, says Ram Sinha from the Pride Circle. Ram discusses some features of the LGBT+ community which distinguish it from other types of minority groups and points to a further challenge of a lack of standardization. Discussing MNC hiring policies related to DEI, to how sexuality is often overlooked within organizations, Ram shares his was experience in the DEI space through several examples of best practices which highlight how emerging markets, like India, are rapidly becoming hotbeds of DEI innovation. Perhaps most striking within his interview is Ram's observation that: "DEI is all about empathy and listening to other perspectives (not just the perspectives of others). Listening to a perspective that is not part of my reality, which is something I don't know about. Hence, that is why I am listening to someone else's perspective."

References

Badgett, M. V. L., Waaldijk, K., & van der Meulen Rodgers, Y. 2019. The relationship between LGBT inclusion and economic development: Macro-level evidence. World Development, 120(8): 1–14.

Banerjee, S. B. 2022. Decolonizing management theory: A critical perspective. Journal of Management Studies, 59(4): 1074–1087.

Google Scholar

Bruton, G. D., Zahra, S. A., Van de Ven, A. H., & Hitt, M. A. 2022. Indigenous theory uses, abuses, and future. Journal of Management Studies, 59(4): 1057–1073.

Carter, A. B., & Phillips, K. W. 2017. The double-edged sword of diversity: Toward a dual pathway model. Social & Personality Psychology Compas, 11(5): e12312.

Doh, J. P. 2021. Distance as diversity: Two sides of the same coin? Journal of Management Studies, 58(6): 1640–1643.

Ely, R. J., & Thomas, D. A. 2020. Getting serious about diversity: Enough already with the business case. Harvard Business Review, 98(6): 68–77.

Gardberg, N. A., Newburry, W., Hudson, B. A., & Viktora-Jones, M. 2022. Adoption of LGBT-inclusive policies: Social construction, coercion, or competition? Social Forces. https://doi.org/10.1093/sf/soac033.

Georgiadou, A., Gonzalez-Perez, M. A., & Olivas-Luján, M. R. (Eds.). 2019a. Diversity with diversity management: Country-based perspectives. Bingley, UK: Emerald Group Publishing Limited. https://doi.org/10.1108/s1877-6361201921.

Georgiadou, A., Gonzalez-Perez, M. A., & Olivas-Luján, M. R. (Eds.). 2019b. Diversity with diversity management: Types of Diversity in organizations. Bingley, UK: Emerald Group Publishing Limited. https://doi.org/10.1108/s1877-6361201922.

Gulati, R. 2022. Deep Purpose: The Heart and Soul of High-Performance Companies. New York, NY: Harper Business/HarperCollins Publishers.

Hermans, M., Newburry, W., Alvarado-Vargas, M. J., Baldo, C. M., Borda, A., et al. 2017. Attitudes towards women's career advancement in Latin America: The moderating impact of perceived company international proactiveness. Journal of International Business Studies, 48(1): 90–112.

Kobrin, S. J. 2020. How globalization became a thing that goes bump in the night. Journal of International Business Policy, 3(3): 280–286.

Koveshnikov, A., Tienari, J., & Piekkari, R. 2019. Gender in international business journals: A review and conceptualization of MNCs as gendered social spaces. Journal of World Business, 54(1): 37–53.

Lumineau, F., Hanisch, M., & Wurtz, O. 2021. International management as management of diversity: Reconceptualizing distance as diversity. Journal of Management Studies, 58(6): 1644–1668.

Moeller, M., & Maley, J. F. 2018. MNC Considerations in identifying and managing LGB expatriate stigmatization. International Journal of Management Reviews, 20(2): 325–342.

Morgan, G., & Kristensen, P. H. 2006. The contested space of multinationals: Varieties of institutionalism, varieties of capitalism. Human Relations, 59(11): 1467–1490.

Rašković, M. 2021. (Social) identity theory in an era of identity politics: Theory and practice. AIB Insights, 21(2). https://doi.org/10.46697/001c.13616.

Sandbu, M. 2020. The Economics of Belonging: A Radical Plan to Win Back the Left Behind and Achieve Prosperity for All. Princeton, NJ: Princeton University Press. https://doi.org/10.1515/9780691204536.

Shoham, A. 2019. Grammatical gender marking: The gender roles mirror. AIB Insights, 19(4): 16–19.

Stahl, G. K., Tung, R. L., Kostova, T., & Zellmer-Bruhn, M. 2016. Widening the lens: Rethinking distance, diversity, and foreignness in international business research through positive organizational scholarship. Journal of International Business Studies, 47(6): 621–630.

Thomas, D. A., & Ely, R. J. 1996. Making differences matter: A new paradigm for managing diversity. Harvard Business Review, 74(5): 79–90.

Vaara, E., Tienari, J., & Koveshnikov, A. 2021. From cultural differences to identity politics: A critical discursive approach to national identity in multinational corporations. Journal of Management Studies, 58(8): 2052–2081.

Zanakis, S. H., Newburry, W., & Taras, V. 2016. Global Social Tolerance Index and multi-method country rankings sensitivity. Journal of International Business Studies, 47(4): 480–497.

Periodical and Internet Sources Bibliography

The following articles have been selected to supplement the diverse views presented in this chapter.

Matthew Alemu, "DEI can work. We just need to end 'cancel culture' first," *Detroit Free Press*, March 29, 2024. https://www.freep.com/story/opinion/contributors/2024/03/29/dei-cancel-culture-privilege-diversity-equality-inclusion-ban/72878066007.

Mahzarin Banaji and Frank Dobbin, "Why DEI Training Doesn't Work—and How to Fix It," the *Wall Street Journal*, September 17, 2023. https://www.wsj.com/business/c-suite/dei-training-hr-business-acd23e8b.

Theo Francis and Lauren Weber, "The Legal Assault on Corporate Diversity Efforts Has Begun," the *Wall Street Journal*, August 8, 2023. https://www.wsj.com/us-news/law/diversity-equity-dei-companies-blum-2040b173.

Mike Gonzalez, "The Biden administration's relentless DEI push continues apace," the *Washington Examiner*, April 8, 2024, www.washingtonexaminer.com/restoring-america/equality-not-elitism/2955477/the-biden-administrations-relentless-dei-push-continues-apace.

Shaun Harper, "Charlamagne tha God's Misinformed, Unhelpful Generalizations About DEI," *Forbes*, April 5, 2024. https://www.forbes.com/sites/shaunharper/2024/04/05/charlamagne-tha-gods-misinformed-unhelpful-generalizations-about-dei.

Dieter Holger, "The Business Case for More Diversity" the *Wall Street Journal*, October 26, 2019. https://www.wsj.com/articles/the-business-case-for-more-diversity-11572091200.

Lindsay Rainbow, "I'm a Black Woman Working in DEI—Here's How I Protect My Peace," the Everygirl, February 6, 2024. https://theeverygirl.com/peace-working-in-dei.

Jathon Sapsford, "Republican Attorneys General Warn Top U.S. Businesses Over 'Discrimination,'" the *Wall Street Journal*, July 14, 2023. https://www.wsj.com/articles/republican-attorneys-general-warn-top-u-s-businesses-over-discrimination-1eb78d29.

Taylor Telford, "Critics of Corporate Diversity Efforts Emerge Even as Initiatives Falter," the *Washington Post*, April 1, 2023.

https://www.washingtonpost.com/business/2023/04/01/woke-capitalism-esg-dei-climate-investment/.

Taylor Telford, "2024 might be do-or-die for corporate diversity efforts. Here's why." the *Washington Post*, December 27, 2023. https://www.washingtonpost.com/business/2023/12/27/dei-affirmative-action-legal-challenges-corporate-america.

Andrew Thurston, "Are Diversity, Equity, and Inclusion Initiatives Helping Workers—or Dividing Them?" the *Brink*, November 28, 2023. https://www.bu.edu/articles/2023/are-diversity-equity-and-inclusion-initiatives-helping-workers.

For Further Discussion

Chapter 1
1. According to the viewpoint by Kristen Parisi, what do you think is driving criticisms of DEI from people like Elon Musk?
2. According to the viewpoint by Sheryl Nance-Nash, how do DEI programs place an additional burden on workers of color? Based on what you've read in viewpoints in this chapter, what could be done to improve this?
3. Based on what you've read in this chapter, what strategies and characteristics can help a workplace DEI program have the best chance of success?

Chapter 2
1. Based on the viewpoints you've read in this chapter, do DEI programs benefit all marginalized groups equally? Why or why not?
2. What are some of the challenges to implementing DEI policies mentioned in this chapter?
3. Why do critics say that DEI policies don't actually improve measures of diversity in the workplace?

Chapter 3
1. What legal challenges does DEI currently face, according to the viewpoints in this chapter?
2. Based on what you've read in this chapter, do you think resistance to DEI is fundamentally rooted in racism or other forms of bigotry? Support your answer using evidence from the viewpoints in this chapter.
3. According to the viewpoint by Tatishe Nteta, Adam Eichen, Douglas Rice, Jesse Rhodes, and Justin H. Gross, what's

Diversity, Equity, and Inclusion

wrong with the notion of a "colorblind" society? Do you agree or disagree with their assertion?

Chapter 4

1. According to the viewpoint by Sundiatu Dixon-Fyle, Kevin Dolan, Dame Vivian Hunt, and Sara Prince, many companies have been slow to implement DEI policies. Why is this the case, and what do you think could be done to help with implementing them?
2. According to the viewpoint by Heather Mac Donald, DEI initiatives in higher education are flawed in part because they set racially diverse students up for academic failure. Do you have any ideas for what could be done to prevent this from being an issue?
3. According to the viewpoints in this chapter, what is the connection between globalization and DEI?

Organizations to Contact

The editors have compiled the following list of organizations concerned with the issues debated in this book. The descriptions are derived from materials provided by the organizations. All have publications or information available for interested readers. The list was compiled on the date of publication of the present volume; the information provided here may change. Be aware that many organizations take several weeks or longer to respond to inquiries, so allow as much time as possible.

American Council on Education
One Dupont Circle NW
Washington, DC 20036
(202) 939-9300
website: www.acenet.edu/

A century-old non-profit organization, the American Council on Education does public advocacy work on behalf of colleges in the country promoting diversity, such as publishing reports on the subject like its 2019 and 2020 "Race and Ethnicity in Higher Education: A Status Report." Per the group's website, this report makes "the case for why race still matters in American higher education."

Anita Borg Institute for Women and Technology
2108 N. St. #8268
Sacramento, CA 95816
(650) 352-7500
email: GHC@anitab.org
website: https://anitab.org/

A network for women and nonbinary people in the tech space, the Anita Borg Institute for Women and Technology offers memberships for people networking in that space. According to its website, the group looks toward "a future where the people who imagine and build technology mirror the people and societies for whom they build it."

Diversify Our Narrative

email: inquiries@diversifyournarrative.com
website: https://diversifyournarrative.com/

Diversify Our Narrative is a student-led 501(c)3 non-profit that aims "to empower tomorrow's change-makers and build an anti-racist future through education nationwide." The group does this by publishing digestible infographics on social justice issues among other activities, which they share with their large social media following.

Government Alliance on Race and Equity (GARE)

email: gare@raceforward.org
website: www.racialequityalliance.org/home

The Government Alliance on Race and Equity is a national network of government working to achieve racial equity and advance opportunities for all. It's a joint project of the Othering & Belonging Institute, which is run by the University of California, Berkeley, and a group called Race Forward.

National Association of Diversity Officers in Higher Education (NADOHE)

1050 Connecticut Ave. N.W., Ste. 500
Washington, DC 20036
(800) 793-7025
email: info@nadohe.org
website: www.nadohe.org

This Washington, D.C.-based non-profit calls itself "the preeminent voice for chief diversity officers." It counts some 2,200 of these among its members, per its website. Founded by William Harvey, an executive in the non-profit space, in 2003, this outfit began as a database and a listserv for chief diversity officers that started holding meetings and conferences in 2005.

National Association for Equity, Diversity & Inclusion (NAEDI)

website: www.naedi.org

This non-profit group calls itself "the premier forum and go-to for convening Equity, Diversity & Inclusion leaders across sectors," according to its website. In addition to that, the group's website tracks trends in the DEI space.

The National Center for Faculty Development and Diversity (NCFDD)

(313) 347-8485
email: help@ncfdd.org
website: www.ncfdd.org/

A small company based in downtown Detroit, the NCFDD provides virtual workshops, coaching, and intensive mentoring resources. Its mission is changing the face of power in academia.

National Center for Institutional Diversity (NCID)

530 E. Liberty Street
Ann Arbor, MI 48104
(734) 764-6497
email: ncidinfo@umich.edu
website: https://lsa.umich.edu/ncid

Operated by the University of Michigan, this group has its origins in the school's longstanding affirmative action admissions policy, which was legally challenged in a number of high-profile Supreme Court cases in the early 2000s. In response, the school formed this group in 2005, which they say is a "means of coalescing local and national efforts to diversify higher education and society." Out of this aim, they say they are building "intergenerational communities

Diversity, Equity, and Inclusion

of scholars and leaders to integrate" what they call "evidence-based approaches in addressing contemporary issues in a diverse society."

National Diversity Council
PO Box 671461
Dallas, TX 75267
(281) 975-0626
website: https://nationaldiversitycouncil.org

This non-profit was started in 2008 and is one of the oldest non-profit diversity, equity, inclusion and belonging organizations in the United States. The council operates as a sort of umbrella organization for a number of statewide and regional chapters and affiliates. The groups aim to foster an understanding of DEIB as a dynamic strategy for success and community well-being through various initiatives.

National Implicit Bias Network
Equal Justice Society
1939 Harrison St., Ste. 818
Oakland, CA 94612
website: https://implicitbias.net

This group is one of the country's leading resources and voices on implicit bias and claims to track the phenomenon's interaction with structural racism and the resulting inequality in areas such as the legal system, law enforcement, education, employment, and housing. The group runs various trainings on this subject and counts various academics and lawyers among its network members.

Partners in Diversity
121 S.W. Salmon St., Ste. 1440
Portland, OR 97204
(503) 552-6765
email: hello@partnersindiversity.org
website: www.partnersindiversity.org

Operating in the larger Pacific Northwest, Partners in Diversity operates educational programs, a career center and resources for CEOs, human resources professionals and diversity influencers, per their website, which says these programs are about "achieving and empowering a workforce that reflects the area's rapidly changing demographics." In addition to this, they also conduct regular scientific research that informs the ways in which the area's employers can successfully diversify and retain multicultural talent.

The Society for Diversity
1 (800) 764-3336
email: info@societyfordiversity.org
website: www.societyfordiversity.org

This group was started in 2009 and calls itself the leading professional association for diversity, equity, inclusion, and accessibility, according to the group's website. It operates the Institute for Diversity Certification, which bestows awards like "Certified Diversity Professional" and "Certified Diversity Executive."

Bibliography of Books

Alison Ash Fogarty and Lily Zheng. *Gender Ambiguity in the Workplace: Transgender and Gender-Diverse Discrimination.* Santa Barbara, CA: ABC-CLIO, 2018.

Mahzarin R. Banaji and Anthony G. Greenwald. *Blindspot: Hidden Biases of Good People.* New York, NY: Delacorte Press, 2013.

Rohit Bhargava and Jennifer Brown. *Beyond Diversity: 12 Non-Obvious Ways to Build a More Inclusive World.* Washington, DC: Ideapress Publishing, 2021.

Jennifer Brown. *Inclusion: Diversity, the New Workplace and the Will to Change.* Hartford, CT: Publish Your Purpose Press, 2016.

Geoffrey L. Cohen. *Belonging: The Science of Creating Connection and Bridging Divides.* New York, NY: W. W. Norton & Company, 2022.

Shirley Davis. *Diversity, Equity & Inclusion for Dummies.* Hoboken, NJ: John Wiley & Sons, 2022.

La'Wana Harris. *Diversity Beyond Lip Service: A Coaching Guide for Challenging Bias.* Oakland, CA: Berrett-Koehler Publishers, 2019.

Heather Mac Donald. *Diversity Delusion.* New York, NY: Griffin, 2020.

Alida Miranda-Wolff. *Cultures of Belonging: Building Inclusive Organizations that Last.* New York, NY: HarperCollins Leadership, 2022.

Pamela Newkirk. *Diversity Inc.: The Failed Promise of a Billion-Dollar Business.* New York, NY: Bold Type Books, 2019.

Symone D. Sanders. *No, You Shut Up: Speaking Truth to Power and Reclaiming America.* New York, NY: Harper, 2020.

Bethaney Wilkinson. *The Diversity Gap: Where Good Intentions Meet True Cultural Change*. Nashville, TN: HarperCollins Leadership, 2021.

Joan Williams. *Bias Interrupted: Creating Inclusion for Real and for Good*. Boston, MA: Harvard Business Review Press, 2021.

Mary-Frances Winters and Mareisha N. Reese. *We Can't Talk about That at Work!: How to Talk about Race, Religion, Politics, and Other Polarizing Topics*. Oakland, CA: Berrett-Koehler Publishers, 2024.

Arthur Woods and Susanna Tharakan. *Hiring for Diversity: The Guide to Building an Inclusive and Equitable Organization*. Hoboken, NJ: John Wiley & Sons, 2021.

Lily Zheng. *DEI Deconstructed: Your No-Nonsense Guide to Doing the Work and Doing It Right*. Oakland, CA: Berrett-Koehler Publishers, 2023.

Lily Zheng and Inge Hansen. *The Ethical Sellout: Maintaining Your Integrity in the Age of Compromise*. Oakland, CA: Berrett-Koehler Publishers, 2019.

Index

A

Abel, Martin, 84–88
Ackman, Bill, 22
affinity group, 57–59
affirmative action, 14, 22, 31, 85, 87, 93–96, 121
age/ageism, 21, 32, 50–55, 60, 84, 86, 117
Alabama, 113
America First Legal Foundation, 22
Arbery, Ahmaud, 25
Aruliah, Natasha, 29

B

Black Lives Matter, 15, 25–26, 109
Blum, Edward, 96
Bright, Marcus, 98–103
Bullock, Dion, 28
Burger, Rulof, 84–85
Burrows, Charlotte, 95

C

Carter-Rogers, Katelynn, 35–39
Castilla, Emilio, 75
Chow, Rosalind, 27
Colakoglu, Saba S., 149–160
Cook, Mike, 76
corporations, 15, 18, 92–95, 114, 127–136

Alaska Airlines, 96
Bank of America Merrill Lynch, 64, 77
Coca-Cola, 73
Deloitte, 76–77
Facebook, 77
Google, 77
Hershey, 96
Home Depot, 22
Kellogg's, 22, 96
Merrill Lynch, 64
Morgan Stanley, 64
Nike, 22
Nordstrom, 22
Smith Barney, 64
Snap, 22
Starbucks, 21
Swift & Company, 67
Tesla, 22–23
Unilever, 22
X/Twitter, 20
Cox, Spencer, 115

D

Daniels, Shereen, 25–26, 28–29
DeSantis, Ron, 98–99
disability, 21, 51, 55–56, 79–83, 150
discrimination, 61, 64, 68–69, 73, 80–81, 84–88, 94, 99, 102–103, 114, 127, 142, 144, 147–148, 150

Index

diversity, equity, and inclusion (DEI)
  backlash, 19–21, 31, 37, 50, 52, 92–123
  cost of, 15, 105, 141
  officers/leaders, 15, 24–29, 31, 50, 57–58, 67, 77, 94–95, 105–111, 113
  outcomes, 63–78, 106, 110–111, 128–137, 150
Dixon-Fyle, Sundiatu, 128–136
Dobbin, Frank, 63–78
Dolan, Kevin, 128–136

E

education, 15, 31, 52, 55, 57, 68, 70, 72–75, 77, 86–87, 92, 94–95, 99–100, 102–111, 113–123, 127, 137–141
Eichen, Adam, 112–117
Eisenhower, Dwight D, 14, 73
emotional labor, 24–29
Engelbert, Cathy, 76
Equal Opportunity Commission, 69
ethnicity, 15, 41, 44, 50–51, 53–56, 59–61, 70, 80, 86, 100, 109, 114–115, 128, 130–136, 150

F

Farber, Reya, 142–148
Feldman, Noah, 95
Florida, 15, 98–103, 113–114
Floyd, George, 15, 25, 31, 48, 94, 114–115
Foundation for Individual Rights and Expression, 108–109
free speech, 104–111
Friedman, Stephen, 79–83

G

Gay, Claudine, 113
gender/sexism, 15, 20–21, 32, 41, 43–44, 50–61, 64–72, 74–77, 80, 82, 84, 86, 99–100, 109, 115, 117, 127–128, 130–136, 140, 142–148, 150, 152–154
Generation Valuable Program, 82
gig economy, 82
Gonzalez-Perez, Maria Alejandra, 149–160
Gorsuch, Neil, 95
government (U.S.), 14, 32
Graham, Stacie CC, 27
Grant, Heidi, 40–44
Greene, Jay, 106–107
grievance procedures, 69–70, 75
Gross, Justin H., 112–117

H

health, 142–148
Heritage Foundation, 106
hiring tests, 64–65, 67–68, 75
Hirschfeld, Magnus, 146
H1-B visa, 102
housing, 88, 102–103, 144
Hsu, Andrea, 93–97
Hunt, Dame Vivian, 128–136

I

immigration, 14, 99, 101–102, 150, 155
Inclusion Institute, 27
Institute for Sexual Science, 146
intersectionality, 127, 149–160
Isdell, Neville, 73

J

Jim Crow, 102
Johnson, Lyndon B., 14
Johnson, Tara, 26
Jorgensen, Christine, 146

K

Kalev, Alexandra, 63–78
Kennedy, John F., 14
Kepinski, Lisa, 27
Krauss, Lawrence, 106

L

laws, 80
  Civil Rights Act, 14
  DEI bans, 15, 98–99, 101–102, 106, 110, 113–115
lawsuits, 15, 18, 21–22, 63–65, 67–68, 73
Levine, Bonnie, 95–96

M

Mac Donald, Heather, 137–141
Marcus, Bernard, 22
marriage, 21

McCracken, Douglas, 76
Men, Rita, 30–34
mentorship, 72–76, 82
Miller, Stephen, 22, 96
Minbaeva, Dana, 149–160
Minkin, Rachel, 49–62
Moore, Antonio, 101
Musk, Elon, 19–23
Myers, Verna, 151

N

Nance-Nash, Sheryl, 24–29
NeuroLeadership Institute, 94
Newburry, William, 149–160
Nteta, Tatishe, 112–117

P

Parisi, Kristen, 19–23
Paul, James, 106–107
performance ratings, 68–69, 75
Phillips, Katherine, 42
politics, 21, 84, 117
  conservative/Republican, 19, 31, 49, 51–53, 55–59, 61–62, 86, 93–95, 101–102, 104–106, 108–110, 113, 115–116, 122
  liberal/Democrat, 49, 51–53, 55–59, 61–62, 105, 108–109, 113
pregnancy/parenting, 21, 57
Pride Circle, 154
Prince, Sara, 128–136

Index

R

race/racism, 14, 20–21, 24–29, 32–33, 41–42, 44, 49–57, 59–62, 64–77, 80, 84–88, 94–96, 98–102, 108–109, 112–123, 127, 137–141, 150, 154–155

Rainbow Disruption, 22

Rašković, Matevž "Matt," 149–160

Rhodes, Jesse, 112–117

Rice, Douglas, 112–117

Rivera, Lauren, 68

Robert Wood Johnson Foundation, 144

Rock, David, 28–29, 40–44

Rufo, Christopher, 113

S

salary transparency, 50, 57, 75

Sam, Jarvis, 22–23

Sandbu, Martin, 151

Sasso, Thomas, 29

Scarritt, Arthur, 118–123

sexual orientation, 21, 32, 50–51, 53–55, 80, 82, 99, 107–108, 115, 138, 143, 148, 150, 152–154

Smith, Steven, 35–39

Stouffer, Samuel, 73–74

Stovall, Janet, 94, 96–97

Supreme Court (U.S.), 15, 22, 31, 94–96

T

Tabvuma, Vurain, 35–39

Taylor, Breonna, 25

Texas, 113

Thomas, David, 72

Thomas, R. Roosevelt Jr., 66

Trump, Donald, 22, 96, 99, 101

U

Utah, 113, 115

W

Waller, Kathy, 73

Wallsten, Kevin, 104–111

Winch, Gil, 83

Diversity, Equity, and Inclusion